Scary Spring
Our Polio Fright of 1955

By C.A. Hartnell

Hawk Prints
HENDERSON, NV

The Adventures of Pete and Carol Ann
SCARY SPRING: Our Polio Fright of 1955
Copyright 2010 by C.A. Hartnell

Hawk Prints
c/o Hartnell House Publishing, LLC
Henderson, Nevada

Front cover illustration by Larry Ruppert
Back cover & interior illustrations by Scott Carter/Stith Printing Inc.
Graphic Design by Aaron & Michelle Grayum / www.thegrayumbrella.com
Author photo by Jim Dorsey

Editorial team:
Cherish Sears, Senior Editor; Cathy Griffith; Becky Barnes; Donna Binion

Library of Congress Cataloging-in-Publication Data

Good Humor-Bryers trademarks used with permission.
Scripture quoted from the King James Version of the Holy Bible.

Manufactured in the United States of America.

Bethany Press International
6820 W 115th St. Bloomington, MN 55438
June 2010

Visit us on the web:
www.hawkprints.com
www.hawksride.com

ISBN 978-1-936119-19-6

*This book is dedicated to all polio victims everywhere
and their families, including my own three family members
who suffered with polio.*

Thank you for your extraordinary courage.

*My sincere thanks to my aunt and uncle,
Dr. Ruth McCammon and Dr. Charles McCammon,
for the research they did on the polio vaccine.*

Contents

Prologue

Dr. Jonas Salk's polio vaccine began its first field trial in April of 1954. Seven hundred thousand first, second, and third graders lined up to receive the vaccine. Americans began to hope that Dr. Salk's vaccine would cure polio. But, one year later, in 1955, a disaster occurred. The vaccine, made by Cutter Laboratories in Berkeley, California, contained live poliovirus. This contaminated vaccine affected children in several states. Two hundred four children became infected with polio from the bad batch of vaccine. Over 150 kids were paralyzed and eleven died.

The terrible disease of polio caused suffering for adults and children across the United States and around the world. Carol Ann's connection to polio, Cutter Laboratories, and the polio vaccine began on the first day of April 1955.

Chapter One

April First

Plink. Plink. Ping.

The familiar sound sent shivers down my spine. *Yikes! Which unlucky kid in our family is getting a shot?* I thought. *Could this be the start of a scary spring?*

Metal needles and glass tubes pinged inside of a stained cooking pot on the stovetop. Like stiff spaghetti they bobbed up and down in the boiling water. Steam drifted to the ceiling. A pink crocheted potholder draped across the shot pot's handle. My Aunt Ruthie stood at her kitchen sink while an April breeze fluttered the window curtains.

I pressed my back against the wall. *Yikes! I'm eleven-years-old and still afraid of shots. I* hate *shots.* I took a deep breath...no rattle. I felt my forehead...no fever. I swallowed...no sore throat. *Sniff. Sniff. Sniff.* No stuffy nose. *Whew. I'm okay, so I'm not the one getting a shot.* I grabbed my school bag and walked slowly into the steamy kitchen.

My tall and beautiful aunt, Dr. Ruth McCammon, looked more like a movie star than a doctor. Her printed dress was tucked in snuggly at the waist. A crisp, white apron pressed down the dress' flared skirt. Aunt Ruthie smoothed a strand of her auburn hair then walked over to the stove to check on her shot pot. *Yikes. I hate shots!*

My aunt worked at the stovetop. *She's my dad's only sister and she's not afraid of shots. Dad's proud that she's a medical doctor and a pathologist. That's a doctor who studies the symptoms of a disease*, I remembered. *I'm proud of her, too.* She turned around and smiled at me as if she heard my thoughts.

"Hi, Aunt Ruthie," I said then asked, "Is someone sick?"

"Hello, Carol Ann. Don't get near Jimmie. He's sick with strep throat. He needs some medicine to make him feel better," said my aunt.

I saw a movement at the kitchen table. Granny Mary cradled 2-year-old Jimmie across her lap. Green, gooey stuff oozed from his scabby nose. He whimpered then turned his gunky face into Granny's blue gingham sleeve. *Yuck. Poor little guy.*

"If I hear the ice cream man, do you want me to buy you an ice pop?" I asked. Cousin Jimmie nodded his feverish head up and down like a puppet.

"Thank you, Carol Ann. That's very thoughtful," said Aunt Ruthie, as she turned off the burner under her crusty, old, shot pot. Steam rose up and circled her face.

"See you later," I said, then I cut out of there before I witnessed an *injection*. That's what Aunt Ruthie called a shot. When the shot pot was on the stove, that signaled the time to get out and get out fast!

In the yard, I listened for the tinkling tunes of the ice

cream man's truck. Jimmie needed an ice pop so he'd feel better. He also needed some courage. *I wish my good friend Pete could talk to him. An old shot pot wouldn't scare Pete. He's the same age as me, but he's not afraid of anything. Even as a little kid he always ran around in a red, homemade cape with black lettering on it that spelled out* **KID COURAGEOUS.** *I wish I could have courage like Pete.*

I looked around the yard. *Where is Pete, anyway?* Afternoon air ruffled my newly bobbed, brown hair. The cut ends tickled my neck. I tucked a stray strand behind my ear as I walked into the yard.

"Owwwwwwwww!" screamed cousin Jimmie through the open kitchen window. I crossed my arms to grab my thin shoulders. *Ouch. Poor Jimmie.*

"Carol Ann, Carol Ann, Carol Ann," called my younger sisters and cousins from the play yard. "Climb with us," they begged.

The kids crawled on the monkey bars like a bunch of...monkeys. My sisters, Kathleen and Gail, climbed with our six-year-old cousin Cathie. Seven-year-old Mandy Hawking, from next door, climbed around, too. I smiled at them and their limber arms and legs that swung from bar to bar. Our cousin, Little Charlie, slid down a pole then plopped on the ground. He scrambled back up so he could hang upside down. His blond hair waved earthward.

Up. Up. Up. I climbed the stamped metal steps of our tall slide. My hands gripped the cold, steel railings and hauled me to the top...the top of the world. Puffy clouds floated across the blue sky. With my skirt tucked under me, down, down, down I slid. My bangs flew straight up then flowed like a waterfall across my forehead.

What a kick! That was a lot of fun! Quickly, I climbed back up the slide's steps. Up on top again, I looked down into Pete's yard. The Hawking's house sat on the front of their lot with a garage and workshop at the back. *Where is Pete, anyway?*

Pete's older brother, John Hawking, was standing next to the garage. His friends called him "Hawk." The girls called him "The Most" and "Dreamy." Hawk was talking to his friends, Ernie and Tim. Blond-haired Tim wiped red paint off of his arm as he balanced on his crutches. As a kid, he had polio. Finally, I spotted Pete's brown crew cut as he walked past his sixteen-year-old brother, John, and the other teens. Pete looked up. I waved. He waved back.

"Hey, Pete, walk over if you can!" I yelled.

"I'll ask my mom!" he yelled back as he ran to his house.

"Carol Ann, Carol Ann, Carol Ann," the younger kids called up to me where I sat on the slide. Their chorus startled me. I looked down at five grimy faces. "Play hide and seek with us," they begged. "You can hide first."

"Not today, kids," I said. "I'm waiting for Pete to walk over. Ask Uncle Charlie to play some games with you when he gets home today from working at the hospital."

"But what about playing hot potato?" asked my younger sister Kathleen. "Or Simon says? Or mother may I? Or what about dodge ball? That's your favorite!"

"I looked down at the kids and said, "I'll play dodge ball if Pete wants to."

"Yeah, let's play dodge ball!" said Little Charlie.

"Who's got the dodge ball?" asked Pete as he walked through the gate between our yards. He stood at the end of the slide and used his hands to shade his brown, intelligent eyes. He asked, "Are you having fun up there? You wanna play some dodge ball?"

"Sure." I stiffened my shoulders then slid, *whooooooooosh*, down the slick slide. My world rushed past me. On the ground again, I straightened my skirt and blouse.

"The last one left in the game is the winner," said Pete as Little Charlie handed him the ball. We scrambled to the end of the grassy area next to the sidewalk. The little kids pushed and pulled at each other to hide behind me so they wouldn't get hit. Pete lifted the ball, moved back his arm, and *whaaaam* flew the ball in my direction. I dodged to the right as the ball flew past me and thumped Gail on the leg.

"Gail, you're out!" yelled Pete. "You're next, Carol Ann."

One by one the kids were knocked out of the game and sat down on the sidelines. Now it was only me. Pete slammed the ball to my left, then over my head, then next to my knee. I dodged every pitch. Pete wound up a great toss and let it go. The dodge ball flew at me, but so did a black, tan, and white ball of fur! I stooped down to dodge Pete's pitch and got hit by a...puppy! He wagged his white-tipped tail against my shirt as I stood up with him.

"Where do you belong?" I asked the pup as Pete and the kids crowded around me.

"Let us see him, Carol Ann," chorused the kids. "Okay, I'll put him down if you sit down and don't pick him up." I kneeled down so they could crowd around the pint-sized puppy. They petted his tan and white head, felt his floppy ears, rubbed the short fur on his black back, and tickled his white tummy. When the puppy turned over, his short, white legs kicked wildly.

Pete kneeled next to me and said, "Cute Beagle pup.

Looks just like my grandpa's dog. I watched him run across your yard from back there." Pete pointed to Mr. Chester's yard behind our back fence.

"Mr. Chester is the mean old man who lives behind us. Yikes," I said.

"Let me have the pup, kids, so I can take him home." Pete picked up the pup and cradled him in his arms. Loud rock and roll music blared over the fence. The pup's ears jerked up to listen. Lucky Pete had a yard full of teens helping Hawk restore his old car.

Tim painted while Ernie hopped-up the engine. The teens worked together as a team. "Fire it up!" someone yelled. "Punch it!" An engine roared really loud.

BRUMMM, BRUMMM, BRUMMM.

"My brother turned an old car into a hot rod," said Pete. "It's a 1937 Ford two-door sedan with a slant back and chopped top. That car's so cherry...you know, neat. Hawk's friends helped him fix it up like new. They replaced the old, 60-horsepower stock engine with a Ford Flathead V8. Hawk and Ernie and Tim are so hip...you know, with it. They drive cool roads like Route 66. They see the latest movies at El Monte Drive-in. And they cruise to Dan's Diner to get burgers with fries and triple thick chocolate shakes."

"You're lucky to have a hip older brother who works on cars," I said.

"Did you hear the latest, Carol Ann?" asked Pete as he patted the puppy. "Our elementary school got picked for the Polio Vaccine Field Trial. Everyone in the school is getting a polio shot next week!"

"Yikes!" I said. The puppy lifted his head to stare at me. "When we get the shot, will we have to stand in a long line with our sleeves rolled up like I saw on TV?" I asked.

"Yep," said Pete. "But what are you worried about? You're a winner, Carol Ann. You just won at dodge ball. You can win at getting a shot."

"That's not true. I'll faint! I'll throw up! I'll run like in dodge ball! Hey, running is a good idea!" My stomach churned. "Puppy, can you teach me to run fast? I hate shots. I hate Aunt Ruthie's shots. And I'll really hate getting a shot from the school nurse."

Pete looked at me and said, "Aw, gee, the school nurse gives good shots when you hold real still."

Then I thought to myself, *polio's worse. It's THE WORST. Polio cripples and kills. Look how it crippled Tim. A shot isn't as bad as getting polio. O God, give me courage.* I prayed. "What day is the vaccine arriving?" I asked.

"APRIL FOOLS!" Pete roared. The puppy bounced on his shaking shoulder.

I frowned at him. "You…!" I sputtered. "What a mean April first trick!"

"No, a great trick! I fooled you good on April Fools' Day! You should have seen your face, Carol Ann. A storm cloud crossed it." He laughed some more, "Ha, ha, ha."

"That polio vaccine is really scary, Pete. You shouldn't tease about getting a shot," I scolded him. "Awhile ago, poor cousin Jimmie got a shot from his mom and he screamed really loud."

"Sorry," said Pete. He looked at the kids crawling on the monkey bars. "First through third graders are getting the trial vaccine." He motioned his head, "Oops, that means kids like those guys. Luckily, our school didn't get picked for Dr. Salk's Field Trial. I don't want to be a 'Polio Pioneer' and get one of the first vaccines."

I looked at his sorry face and said, "You got me good. You fooled me." Sand crunched under our feet as we walked past the monkey bars, the laundry-covered clothesline that smelled like detergent, and then the chicken car that smelled like...chickens. Pete stopped to look back at the chicken car. The pup sniffed.

"Cluck, cluck, cluck," Pete mocked as he flapped one of his arms.

"Don't scare the baby chicks," I warned, "Or the puppy in your arms."

"You're the only family in the world who has a chicken car. That broken-down old car is choked with chickens," laughed Pete. The pup *sniff, sniff, sniffed*.

"They like it here," I said then shrugged. "They flew out of Mr. Chester's yard."

I looked at the rusty old car. It sat in the middle of my yard in a dirt patch under a tree. Shade from the tree kept the grass from growing. Next to the chicken car a long sidewalk snaked from Aunt Ruthie's house to mine. Just then, screaming kids ran around the chicken car, across the sidewalk, and toward the front of the house.

The giggling group made a plan, then scattered in four directions. My sister, Kathleen, leaned against our house, her face pressed in her hands. She shouted, "ONE...TWO...THREE...FOUR...FIVE...SIX...SEVEN...EIGHT...NINE...TEN! READY OR NOT, I'LL FIND YOU!" She turned around to hunt for hidden kids.

I loved playing hide and seek. I was a good hider. Pete had a hard time finding me. I asked him, "You want to play hide and seek or watch the television at my house?"

"Let's watch TV," said Pete. "Does your mom have any homemade cookies?"

"No," I said. "She hasn't baked in a week." Pete's mouth drooped. "APRIL FOOLS! Ha, Ha, I got you!" I laughed out loud. The pup watched my laughing mouth.

"So there might be some cookies?" He looked hopeful as we walked to my house.

"Let's check," I said. "Mom had all her baking stuff out this morning: cookie sheets, spatula, oven mitt, flour, sugar, butter, and chocolate chips."

Squawk, squawk, screech.

We ducked as several chickens flew by our heads. Two more balanced on our bush-covered back fence. Bright green bushes disguised the old chain-link fence between our back yard and Mr. Chester's yard.

"What's going on over there?" Pete asked. "What's that noise?"

"*Shhhhhhh*...I don't know," I whispered, holding my finger to my mouth. "Something scary goes on in Mr. Chester's yard. I've heard awful noises behind those bushes. He's got chickens and watchdogs over there. Maybe the pup is one of them."

"Have you ever seen Mr. Chester?" Pete asked. "My dad has. He said Mr. Chester is crabby, crippled, and cruel."

"I've seen him," I said. "He is crippled. Mom said Mr. Chester got polio in the 1916 Polio Epidemic, but so did Granny Catherine and Great Aunt Julie. They don't act hateful. They're very loving. They send us gifts all the way from Chicago, Illinois. Tim is crippled from polio, but he's still nice."

"You see that pile of dirt over there?" asked Pete. "That's

where the puppy crawled through. We've gotta put him back in his yard," said Pete as he ran to the fence.

I followed Pete like a caboose on a train. He set the puppy down near the corner of the bush-covered fencing. The pup yelped a thank you as he bounced between our ankles. His cute, pink tongue licked my leg while his tiny tail beat the dirt. Pete pushed him gently through the hole under the fence.

"Oh, Pete, he's so cute," I said as we backed away. "Will he be okay?"

"*Shhhhhhh,*" Pete said. He pointed. "Look at that. Is someone playing an April Fools' trick on us?" Behind the bush-covered fence, a gray thatch of hair bobbed along moving in our direction. The hair looked like the scraggly stuff that grew on old Mr. Chester's head. "Back up, Carol Ann, so he won't see us."

"What if the puppy doesn't belong to Mr. Chester after all?" I whispered as I backed up one slow step at a time. "I will keep him if he doesn't have a home."

Up and down, up and down, the head seesawed with each crippled step. Garbled curses flowed nonstop. A dog yelped painfully. The puppy scooted halfway back into my yard. Mr. Chester's spiky hair moved ever closer to us. Only the bushes blocked his view.

"That's no April Fools' trick," I whispered. "That head has Mr. Chester's hair on it. Yikes." I looked down at our fence corner and whispered, "Watch out little puppy."

"Mr. Chester can't see us through the bushes, so don't worry," whispered Pete. "He's bad news. My dad said that polio crippled Mr. Chester's legs and heart. I hope he still has enough heart so he won't hurt that baby Beagle."

Just then a voice yelled out, "Hey pup, where'd you get to? Where are you hiding? I'm tired of chasing you around, you mangy mutt. If you don't watch out, a chicken hawk will swoop down and snatch you out of my yard. Get over here right now!"

The puppy slunk forward under the fence and disappeared from sight as Pete and I slunk backwards. We both turned and sprinted across the grass to my house.

Behind us we heard a stern voice. "There you are!" growled mean old Mr. Chester. "You need to stay away from this rusty old fence, you bad pup."

We stopped and looked back. The spiky gray hair kept moving up and down behind the bushes. Mr. Chester prowled his fence like a mangy, limping, growling, junkyard dog. The bushes swayed and rustled. Then...a gnarled hand slipped through the greenery along the rusty old fence. We jumped out of sight onto my front porch. Even though the fence was over thirty feet away, I held my breath.

Chapter Two

Home Sweet Home

"That looked like a monster's hand," said Pete.

"It was Mr. Chester's hand," I said as my heart pounded like a drum. "He is a monster if he hurts that poor puppy. It's funny that the pup plays hide and seek with Mr. Chester. Wasn't the puppy cute? I wish I could bring him home."

"Yep, he's a cute pup," said Pete.

Mom pushed open the screen door and asked, "Are you playing hide and seek?"

"Yes, we are, Mom. We're hiding from Mr. Chester, and we're hoping he's not seeking us," I answered. Pete nodded his head up and down in agreement.

"That crippled old man is not going to play games with you two. I'm sure he's got better things to do. Would you like a snack?"

"Do we want a snack?" asked Pete sarcastically. "Sure we do!"

I pushed Pete through the open door into our home, sweet home cluttered with toys, sweet toys. Some days, Mom watched soap operas to help her escape the toys and kids' mess.

"Gee, Mrs. H., it looks like you had a tough day at the old homestead. Looks like the kids left a big mess for you to clean up. I sure hope your family appreciates you like I do. I really appreciate your cookies. Is that what I smell?" Pete asked hopefully.

"My cookies!" Mom rushed into her kitchen. The oven door banged open. A cookie sheet clattered on the counter. "I got them in time," Mom called out. "Perfect."

"I'm hungry for one of your mom's perfect cookies," said Pete. "My mouth loves munching cookies. See. It's empty and needs filling."

Pete's mouth hung open. I saw his tonsils and his teeth. "Yuck, Pete. You can close your mouth now, before I start gagging. Maybe I'll start calling you The Munch Mouth of La Madera Avenue."

"Real funny," he said, and then began to follow his nose into the kitchen.

"Just a minute," I said. "Let's clean up the living room 'cause it'll help my mom."

Our living room got really messy really fast with four kids living in our house. Pete piled baby toys back into the toy box. I gathered stuff lying around the room: a sweater, a lunch box, a pair of shoes, a coloring book, and a box of crayons. I peeked over the pile in my arms to see Pete squatting down on the floor.

"You're supposed to put those toys away, Pete, not fiddle with them," I said. "I wonder if Mr. Chester's puppy would like some of my baby brother's toys. We could sneak toys under the fence, but old Mr. Chester might stomp on them with his big boots."

"The puppy needs to stay away from those boots. The pup would like these toys that I'm NOT fiddling with. I'm looking at them. Babies have okay stuff," Pete said. "When I pulled the string on the Buzzy Bee, it clicked, turned its plastic wings, and waved those wiggly wooden balls on its antennae. Hey Pup would like the Buzzy Bee."

"Now what are you talking about, Pete?" I asked. "Who's 'Hey Pup?'"

"That's what Mr. Chester called his puppy," said Pete, "So that's what I named him."

I took a deep breath. "Well, he's not our pup to name," I sighed. "While I work to put this stuff away, you can fiddle a little longer with Mr. Buzzy Bee and its wiggly antennae," I laughed. "If baby Mark crawls in here, you'd better share."

Pete put away the rest of the toys, while I put away the pile in my arms. The room looked tidy now. Dad would be glad. He liked coming home to a clean house. Pete sat down on the sofa and stared into the corner.

"Did you get a brand new RCA color television set?" he asked with excitement.

"My dad brought it home yesterday," I said. "He bought it with a work bonus. The TV cost lots of dollars. Mom said he splurged a month's pay. Isn't it cool?"

"Real cool. You can watch all the good shows in living color. I wish my dad would buy a color TV. Our old black and white set will last forever. Your dad's lucky to bring home a bonus," said Pete. "My dad only brings home car parts from his shop."

"Dad wins lots of prizes as a salesman for Brunswick Corporation," I said. "They make bowling alleys and supplies. In the past, he won a waffle iron, cookware, and an electric corn popper. Dad even got a fancy ring for being Brunswick's top salesman. After work, Dad likes to relax in front of the television set. Watching our new TV will be like going to the movie theater."

"We can eat popcorn and watch our favorite movie stars in cool color," said Pete.

I brushed my hand across the shiny, smooth top of the new television set. The TV's silver screen sat inside of a wooden cabinet. The screen looked like it belonged in a spaceship. Knobs stuck out below the screen and mesh fabric covered the speakers.

"Carol Ann. Pete. Get your snack," Mom called from her kitchen.

Pete followed me into the heart of our home. In Mom's kitchen, white metal cabinets, attached to pale yellow walls, surrounded us. Red marbleized counters, edged in sparkling chrome trim, formed a U-shaped countertop. To my left, Mom's white stove radiated heat. A round clock with skinny black arms *ticked, ticked, ticked* from the stove's back panel.

Shiny baking sheets littered the counter between the kitchen and the eating nook. A plate of freshly baked chocolate chip cookies sat in the middle of our red and chrome kitchen table. Cold milk filled tall, multi-colored aluminum cups called tumblers. Pete grabbed the blue tumbler and gulped down some milk.

"Sit down, Pete. Munch a cookie," I teased as I pulled out a chair. The red vinyl-clad seat squished under me. I reached across the table for a cookie and the red tumbler filled with milk. My mouth savored the tasty treat loaded with melted chocolate. *Yum. Mom's kitchen smells like cookie heaven. Would Hey Pup like to eat a cookie?*

"Thanks, Mrs. H.," Pete said between bites. "Your chocolate chip cookies are the best in the west. Dan at Dan's Diner should put your cookies on his menu."

"Why, thank you, Pete," said Mom.

"Cookies! Mom baked cookies!" yelled my two sisters as they ran into the kitchen and sniffed like puppies. *Sniff, sniff.* I sniffed the heavenly scent once again, too. Five famished youngsters crowded around the table. Grubby hands grabbed for cookies.

"Wait a minute, kids. First, wash your hands," Mom said.

"I'll help them," I offered and walked toward the sink. A yellow glass bowl, cookie ingredients, and measuring cups littered the counter by the stove.

I pulled the step stool up to the kitchen sink. Black rubber skids squeaked on the asphalt tile floor. The kids took turns climbing up the steps to wash their filthy hands. I smelled soap. Mom's homemade white curtains, edged in red calico ruffles, stirred at the open window over the sink. Plaster tulip plaques decorated the walls under the white cabinets. Four, red-topped, tin canisters stored flour, sugar, coffee, and tea. I pushed the canisters back against the wall and swiped a wet dishrag across the counter.

"Carol Ann, Carol Ann," Gail said. "Pwease, pour me a gwass of milk."

"Okay," I said. I picked up Mom's bright blue, aluminum pitcher and poured milk from its no-drip spout into a pink, metal tumbler.

"Carol Ann, Carol Ann. I need more milk, too, pwease,"

mimicked Pete.

He still sat at the table, surrounded by kids. His younger sister, Mandy, snuggled next to him. Pete looked down and patted her pretty, white-blonde curls. He raised his head. He smiled through smeared chocolate chunks that covered his mouth.

"Hee, hee," I giggled. "You should see your face, Pete. It's full of chocolate. Did you eat cookies or rub your face in them?" I asked between giggles.

He grabbed a napkin and wiped his face while I wiped the table. Baby Mark played on the kitchen floor with some plastic bowls. He banged them together and laughed. Mom worked on a beef and noodle casserole for dinner. Heat waves from the stove warmed my legs as I cleaned up. I thought about Aunt Ruthie's shot pot.

"Mom, is it true that there's a shot called a polio vaccine that will stop kids from getting polio?" I asked. "Is Aunt Ruthie working on it?"

"Yes," Mom answered. "There's a doctor named Dr. Jonas Salk in Pittsburgh, Pennsylvania who's been working on a polio vaccine for years now. Aunt Ruthie works with a research team here in California that's helping Dr. Salk. This polio shot will save lots of lives."

"Will the shot give me polio?" I asked.

"Not if the vaccine is carefully made by reputable labs," Mom answered.

"What's rep-u-table?" I questioned.

"That means the lab is trustworthy and will do a good job," Mom said.

"What is polio anyway? How do people get it? Kids at school talk about it all the time. They say that a person gets polio from not washing their hands with soap and water. Gail thinks that kids get polio from falling in the gutter. I heard that we could get polio from swimming in the high school pool. Is that how Tim got polio? Can a puppy get it?"

Mom frowned. "I don't know if a person gets polio from the gutter. Doctors think polio enters the body through the nose or mouth." Mom bent down to put her casserole into the oven. "Polio is a virus that's extremely small. Your Aunt Ruthie told me that the poliovirus causes the disease of polio by infecting healthy cells in the body. The poliovirus causes fever, sore throat, stiff muscles, and paralysis which produces helplessness."

Mom looked at me then finished talking. "I don't think puppies can get polio. The virus infects children more than adults. Most polio breakouts happen in summer and in big cities. I'm glad we live in the country behind our two doctors."

"I'm glad, too," I said. "I'm glad Aunt Ruthie and Uncle Charlie take care of us."

"Pete . . . eeeeeeeee!" yelled Pete's older sister, Mary Jane, from next door. "You and Mandy need to get home before dark!"

A rosy glow filled the sky as I walked Pete and his younger sister home. Gold-tinged clouds reflected the sunset on the western horizon. Some chickens in the chicken car clucked quietly. I stopped to listen for the puppy. I didn't hear him whimpering.

"Do you think the puppy will be okay?" I asked.

"I don't know, Carol Ann," said Pete. "I hope so. Let's check on him tomorrow."

"Meet me early in the morning before we go shopping in

town," I said.

Twelve-year-old Mary Jane stood at the open gate. Her perfect blonde curls cascaded around her pretty oval face. She re-tucked her white blouse into the waistband of her pink pleated skirt. Her outfit looked so cute. One black shoe impatiently tapped the ground. *Uh oh...Mary Jane looks mad. Someone is in trouble. I hope it's not me.*

"Where have you been, Peter James Hawking?" Mary Jane asked angrily. "I've been calling your name for hours. Mom wants you home to set the table for dinner. Then you need to finish the rest of your chores instead of playing games."

"I'm here, Mary Jane. So sorry I upset you. Don't rattle your cage with rage," Pete said to his big sister. Behind his upraised hand, Pete pointed at her with his other hand. He silently mouthed the words, "Party-pooper."

I tightened my mouth to keep from laughing. The name "party-pooper" perfectly described Mary Jane. She liked to break up our fun. *Ting a ling a ling a ling* sounded across the rooftops. The ice cream man's truck drove nearby. I reached into my pocket to jingle some change. I owed Jimmie an ice pop so he would feel better.

"I have to go and catch the ice cream man," I said. "Good night, Mary Jane and Mandy. Good night, Pete. See you later, alligator."

"After while, crocodile," Pete said and waved.

Ting a ling a ling. I raced out to the front yard to catch the ice cream man.

Dark shadows crowded the porch when I walked into Aunt Ruthie's house. She washed dishes at the sink. Aunt Ruthie's six-year-old daughter, Cathie, stood on a step stool by her mom. Round and round cousin Cathie twirled her soapy arms in the dishwater. Mr. Chester's pup could use some swirling soapy water to get clean.

Uncle Charlie patted Cathie and said, "You're doing a fabulous job." He noticed me, waved, and walked out of the kitchen. He was gone and, luckily, so was the shot pot.

"How's Jimmie, Aunt Ruthie? I've got a Root Beer ice pop for him," I said.

"He's sleeping, but he'll enjoy it later," said my aunt. "Thank you for getting it."

"You're welcome," I said with a smile. "Good night." I bent down to pick up my school bag filled with papers, homework, books, and lunch leftovers.

Dangerous darkness waited outside for me. *Yikes.* On the driveway, Dad's car crouched like a menacing monster. Our porch light glowed in the distance on our home. The long sidewalk stretched in front of me. Darkness seemed like an enemy. My favorite movie star, John Wayne, bravely faced all his enemies. *Can I face mine?*

"I'm afraid," I whispered, then tried to gulp down my fear. *If I try really hard, I can run really fast. O God, help me please,* I prayed. *Help me run fast. Help me be brave like John Wayne and my friend, Pete.*

"One, two, three...GO!" I took off running like Ernie's lightning-fast hot rod. My school bag slapped at my side. *Slap, slap, slap.* I raced against what seemed like ten thousand scary shadows. My footsteps pounded the pavement. My heart pounded in my chest. *Da dump, da dump, da dump.* Safe on the porch at last, I gasped for breath.

"Thank you...God...for helping me...run fast," I said between gulps of air.

Squawk, squawk, squawk screeched Mr. Chester's chickens from behind his fence. I stepped off the porch and looked into the black, inky darkness of our backyard. *Woof, yelp, yelp, woof, woof.*

"Is that Mr. Chester's puppy yelping for help?" I whispered to myself. "Is he all alone in the dark? The poor pup is the size of a small chicken. Yikes."

Do chicken hawks hunt at night? Is a chicken hawk watching the pup right now? Is Mr. Chester watching me? Is he hiding in the darkness like a monster...like a chicken hawk? I jumped back onto our porch, pulled open the front door, and jumped inside my home, sweet home. *Screech, squawk, squawk.*

Chapter Three

Downtown In The Tank

"Girls, hurry up," Dad called across the yard. "Let's get rolling."

Through the open front door, I called, "Dad's calling us, Mom. He said to hurry up!" I grabbed Kathleen's and Gail's hands and hurried them toward our two-tone, Dodge Royal, four-door sedan. Dad paced impatiently by the driver's door.

"Mom will be right here," I told him.

"That's what she always says," he said and smiled.

Dad looked handsome in his charcoal gray slacks and gray striped shirt with the button-down collar. His dark brown hair waved back from his forehead. He smelled like spice cologne. He tucked his six-foot, three-inch body onto the driver's seat. I tucked Kathleen and Gail onto the seat behind him.

"Are you girls ready for your shopping spree?" he asked. My sisters nodded their heads and giggled.

Click, click, click.

Mom's high heels clicked toward us on the sidewalk. Mark sat securely on her hip. She wore her favorite black, calf-length skirt with a white crocheted top. The morning breeze ruffled her dark hair. She disappeared into Aunt Ruthie's house to drop Mark off so Granny Mary could watch him.

"Carol Ann," Pete called from the open gate. "I need to ask you something." Pete's Yankee-style baseball uniform and cap looked cool for his game today.

"We're leaving in a minute, Pete. What do you want?" I asked.

"Are you going downtown in The Tank?" he asked.

"Yes and no," I said. "We're going downtown to shop for Easter dresses, but our car *isn't* a tank."

"Okay," he whispered then looked around. "Do me a favor. If you go into the department store, check and see if there are any cowboy wrist watches for sale."

"All right, I'll check," I whispered back. "Do me a favor and check on Hey Pup." I hurried back to the car. Pete loved cowboy stuff. I liked it, too. We both liked watching cowboys and dogs in TV shows like *Lone Ranger, Rin Tin Tin,* and *Lassie.*

Mom and I slid into the car on opposite sides and closed the doors. We were ready to roll! Dad pulled the gearshift into reverse. He looked behind him as he placed his arm over the seat. "Are you girls finally ready to go?" he asked.

"Go, go, go," we chorused from the back seat. The bulky car reversed rapidly for a "Tank." *Is it true what Pete called Dad's car? Is it a tank?* We wiggled wildly as Dad drove through the neighborhood. Then we fidgeted, smiled, smoothed our white gloves, bounced up and down, chattered nonstop, fiddled with our purses, counted money, smiled, smiled, and smiled some more. We sniffed Mom's perfume that smelled like flowers.

As we traveled on Peck Road, Mom warned, "Harry, watch your speed." Dad slowed down the powerful V-8 engine. Dozens of dials illuminated the dashboard.

I rolled my window up and down by cranking the chrome handle. As Dad drove, houses and businesses flashed by us. I saw Dan's Diner, a tire dealership, the local gas station with a red star on its sign, and a mobile home park.

Ernie's '32 is parked in front of El Monte Ford, Inc. Ernie and Hawk must be in there buying car parts for Hawk's old car. I need to ask Pete when Hawk's old Ford car will be completely restored. Dad changed lanes to avoid a ready-mix concrete truck in front of us that was slowing down.

Dad drove The Tank into his favorite gas station. Its sign boasted a red, flying horse. *Will our car fly when Dad fills it with the station's top octane gas?* Dad climbed out of the car to "fill 'er up." A uniformed attendant walked over to help.

"The traffic's terrible this morning on Peck Road," Mom said, as she looked back as us.

"Uncle Charlie's funny," I giggled. "He said Peck Road is like an artery to the downtown shopping area because downtown is the heart of El Monte."

"Charlie's a doctor, so he thinks of everything as body parts," Mom answered. "He's right, though. The downtown is like a heart. The businesses there give life to the town just like a heart gives life to the body. Oh, now I sound like your uncle Charlie!"

A sweet gas smell breezed in through the open window. Gail bounced on the edge of the car's seat. Kathleen fanned out the skirt on her printed dress. Thankfully, we were all wearing different dresses today. A few years ago, Mom dressed us like triplets. *Yuck*.

We watched the cars driving up and down the busy road. I straightened the fingers on my white gloves. Mom's shoulders lifted then fell in a sigh.

"What's wrong, Mom?" I asked. "Are you sad?"

She turned around to look at me. "No, I'm not sad. I'm disappointed."

"Dish…appointed about what?" Gail asked in Gail language.

Mom said, "About California Baptist College moving to Riverside."

"Why?" I asked.

"Because I wanted to take some classes there," Mom said. "The college used to be on Peck Road at the First Southern Baptist Church."

"Wow," I said. "My mom…the college student. That sounds so cool."

"No," she replied. "Your mom…who *wanted* to be a college student."

Dad tapped on the car window and smiled at us. We all smiled back.

"Besides," Mom sighed again, "what would you do without me two days a week? My favorite place is my home, surrounded by my family, working my fingers to the bone, and baking chocolate chip cookies for you and your friend, Pete."

Dad climbed back into the car and started The Tank's engine. He drove around a black Oldsmobile club coupe and a Willys sedan. A flame-painted roadster roared behind us.

"Teens and cars don't mix," Dad said as he shook his head.

Woooooooooooo. We-ah. We-ah. We-ah. Wooooooooooooo. We-ah. We-ah.

Dad pulled over. The siren grew louder and louder. A black and white Cadillac ambulance sped past us transporting a patient somewhere. *Is a polio victim riding to Los Angeles County Hospital where Uncle Charlie and Aunt Ruthie work? Maybe it's racing to the Sister Elizabeth Kenny Polio Hospital on Gillman Road.* I shivered. Iron lungs, braces, crutches, wheelchairs, crippled kids, and lots of pain filled both places. Tim knew about hospitals and pain. *Was Tim ever in an iron lung? I'll have to ask him sometime.*

Dad drove the Dodge tank through traffic to downtown El Monte. Main Street curved in front of us. Tall and short buildings lined both sides of the street. I saw Michael's Men's Store, Seashore Loans, and a department store. I also noticed the grocery store in the distance. On one building, an Air Raid Shelter sign pointed downstairs to a bomb shelter. *I don't ever want to go underground and wait for the city above me to blow up from an atom bomb.* I shivered again. At school, we learned how to duck and cover under our desks for protection.

Dad parked the car on the crowded street. "I'm getting a haircut," said Dad. "I'll pick you up at three o'clock, Jeanne. Don't break the bank by spending all my hard-earned money," Dad laughed as we piled out of The Tank.

"Oh, Harry," Mom giggled. "We girls have a strict budget." Then she turned to us and said, "Let's start in Darla's Dress Shop across the street."

The store window showed spring fashions displayed like a garden of dresses. In contrast, a poster proclaimed, "FIGHT POLIO!" Under the words was a picture of a young girl wearing a white dress. She was using crutches and had monstrous metal leg braces.

She looked like me, I thought. But that poor girl couldn't play, or run, or walk freely down the street on a spring morning. I felt sad for her. Words on the poster said, "Join the March of Dimes." Our family gave money to help. Mom and Aunt Ruthie even walked in a Mother's March. Ernie, Tim, and Hawk put up March posters all over town.

Inside the store, Mom walked back to the girls' section. "Don't touch anything unless you're trying it on," she warned.

Right away I spotted the perfect dress for me hanging on a clothes rack in the corner. I put my gloves into my white vinyl purse. I admired the aqua-blue party dress. A lacy overlay covered the collar and skirt. The matching lace jacket had puffed sleeves. *I love this dress.* Pete would say 'I flipped over it'. What a perfect dress for Easter! The price wasn't so perfect though. I winced at the $12.00 price tag. Mom did, too.

"Carol Ann, the dress you love is four dollars more than I wanted to spend," she said, "but we'll put the dress on hold so we can keep shopping. If we don't find anything else, or I'm able to get your sister's dresses on sale, then maybe we can get it. That's a really big MAYBE."

"Thanks, Mom," I said as I crossed my fingers behind my back for luck.

Back outside on the sidewalk, we walked toward the giant department store. I felt small next to buildings that blocked sunlight from the sidewalk. I looked up at the sign advertising for Dr. D. Silver O.D. He sold glasses. His sign looked like a pair of giant glasses. *Would a pair of glasses help Mr. Chester see the world differently? But if he saw better would it be easier for him to find Hey Pup?* I didn't want him to get glasses.

"Stay by my side, girls, so you don't get lost," Mom said as we entered the department store. "First, let's check the shoe department."

We looked at all the shoes. Mom tried on some beige, stacked-heel pumps, a pair of white, pointed-toe pumps, and cute, tan sandals. Mom loved the sandals. They cost $8.95. Their packaging promised daylong comfort and relaxation for the lady who's always on the go. Mom walked around the shoe department modeling the tan sandals. Those shoes found a spot in the budget. *I hope my dress will find a spot, too.*

As the morning passed, we found everything we needed. Mom bought adorable sale-priced Easter dresses for my sisters, white socks and gloves, some cologne from the fragrance counter, and a blue linen shirt for Dad. While Mom paid for Dad's shirt, I took charge of Kathleen. We walked over by the jewelry counter to look at watches, rings, and other things. A pretty saleslady behind the glass-fronted counter smiled at us then turned away to help another customer.

"You stay next to me, Kathleen, so you don't get lost," I said. I moved along the counter searching for the latest, super duper western wristwatch. When I turned back around, Kathleen had disappeared like magic! *Yikes, I'm in big trouble now!*

"Kathleen," I whispered, "where are you?" The chest-high countertop blocked my view. I couldn't see her anywhere. "Kathleen, answer me." I could see Mom finishing her purchase. I had to find Kathleen and fast. *O God, help me please,* I prayed.

Da dump, da dump, da dump pounded my panicked heart. I ran around the counter. Then I ran around another counter. I spotted Kathleen at the end of it.

Thank you, God, for sparing my short life. Kathleen squatted down near the floor. Her face pressed against the glass. She looked at an assortment of cowboy and western wrist-watches. Pete would be happy. That made me smile. Then I put on my stern face.

"Do you think Mom will buy one of those for me?" Kathleen pointed.

"Mom doesn't buy stuff for girls who don't obey and get lost in department stores," I hissed. I took my white gloves out of my purse. I pulled the gloves onto my shaking fingers.

Mom called, "Let's go have lunch, girls. Thank you for being so well-mannered."

I frowned at Kathleen. She smirked back. I kept her by my side as we crossed four lanes of traffic, walked down the sidewalk, and passed through the drug store. We sat at the counter to order lunch. Losing my sister scared me. *Thank you, God, for helping me find Kathleen,* I prayed. *And please bless our lunch.* I smiled as I bit into my grilled-cheese sandwich. *Yum.* The salty fries with ketchup and a cherry cola calmed me down.

"After lunch, I need a few things here in the drug store. Then we'll buy your dress, Carol Ann," said Mom. "Thank you for minding your sister."

I smiled at Mom's compliment. Then I turned and frowned one last time at Kathleen. She stuck out her tongue and made a raspy noise with it. *Yuck. Kathleen's tongue isn't cute like Hey Pup's.*

We followed Mom around as she checked the things off her shopping list: a baby bib for Mark, a bar of soap, and a compact of pressed-powder make-up. A giant-sized can of roasted peanuts found space on the checkout counter. Mom didn't mind when I put a box of doggie biscuits next to the peanuts. She lets me give treats to the nice dogs in the neighborhood, so I'll slip a few to Hey Pup.

When we walked out of the drug store, I noticed another March of Dimes poster. A young boy who looked like my brother held out his arms wrapped in braces. The caption read, "Lend me a hand." My healthy hands shook my purse as I listened for the sound of loose change. I'd fill my March of Dimes folder and turn it in. That would lend the boy a hand. Hopefully, then, Mark's hands would never need those braces.

At three o'clock sharp, Dad pulled up to the curb just like he said he would. We piled into the car with all our packages. I cradled my Darla's Dress Shop purchase on my lap. Tissue paper rustled around my beautiful dress. I settled back on The Tank's upholstered seat and picked up the box of dog biscuits. The dog picture on the front of the box looked like Hey Pup. *Would he do a trick for a biscuit? Would Mr. Chester let me train his puppy if I asked him nicely? I will pray before I ask Mr. Chester anything.*

"Thank you, Mom and Dad, for my Easter dress. I love it," I said.

"I hope Mom stuck to her budget," Dad said.

Mom smiled as she turned on the radio. Doris Day's soft voice sang, "Secret Love." Mom looked lovingly at Dad as my sisters curled up on the seat next to me. Even though they got lost sometimes, I still loved them. If I owned a puppy and it got lost sometimes, I would still love it, too.

I missed baby Mark, but I was glad he was safe with Granny Mary, who lived with Aunt Ruthie. His healthy hands probably played with toys all day. I didn't want him to get polio like that boy on the poster. *What causes polio? What cures polio? Will Dr. Salk's polio vaccine stop polio? Will my baby brother get polio? Will I get polio this scary spring?* My tired eyes closed. The Tank drove us home.

Chapter Four

Cherrylee School

■▪■▪■▪■▪■▪■▪■▪■▪■▪■▪■▪■

Crunch. Crunch. Crunch.

Four pairs of school shoes shuffled on the edge of La Madera Avenue's gravelly asphalt. I looked down at the speckled street and kicked a stone.

"Hurry up, slow-pokes. We're going to be late for school," Mary Jane scolded in her bossy voice. Her mean words reminded me of Mr. Chester when he called Hey Pup in a mean voice.

Mary Jane walked in front of us. Her no-nonsense steps swayed her navy skirt. Blonde curls bobbed on the collar of her smart-looking sailor blouse. She peered back over her shoulder at us. For the moment, Pete stayed obediently at her side. Every school morning we played follow the leader. Mary Jane was always the leader, and we followed her, but it wasn't a game. Her frowning forehead and mean mouth meant business.

"Peter, stay on the edge of the road like Mom told you," warned Mary Jane as Pete stepped in front of her to kick rocks. *Pop, crunch, pop.*

Giant walnut trees formed a leafy canopy over our heads and into the distance. School kids poured out of low-roofed houses onto La Madera Avenue like waves on the seashore. We passed a black Chevrolet convertible parked on the street.

"Cool car," said Pete as he glanced back at the Chevy automobile. "Hawk's Ford sedan looks as cool as that car. Hawk's friends call his car 'Hawk's Ride.' That's what I'll call it, too."

Mary Jane added, "John bought his 1937 Ford car from our grandpa. The car had a cheap price tag." Mary Jane moved us along like a mother hen with her chicks. Before we crossed Cherrylee Drive, she said, "Look both ways, everyone."

RUMBLE, RUM, RUM. POP. POP.

A black, souped-up, 1932 Ford Hi-boy roadster rolled next to us. Ernie revved his hot rod's engine. Handsome John Hawking leaned out of Ernie's '32.

"What's up, guys?" asked Hawk. "Hey, Pete, Mom asked me to give you this bread." Hawk handed Pete a dollar bill. "You forgot your lunch, kid."

"Com'on, Hawk. Let's split," Ernie whined. "I'm ready to agitate some gravel, so let's leave. Say 'bye, bye' to those ankle-biters."

Hawk laughed and said, "Have a blast in school, guys. See 'ya later."

Ernie punched it. The roaring flathead V8 engine pounded my ears. His car burned rubber down the street. Then it peeled around the corner on the way to El Monte

High School. Burnt tire fumes choked my throat. I pinched my nose closed.

"That car's a screamer," said Pete. "Ernie owns one of the best hot rods at his school."

Mary Jane sighed. "He's so cute, too. Maybe I'll get to ride in Ernie's '32 soon."

I looked at Kathleen and scrunched my nose. We stopped in front of the Bailey house. Tall trees shaded the yard. Red siding with white trim decorated the house. White shutters framed each window. In their yard, curious dirt piles dotted the green grass.

"Why are the Baileys digging up their yard?" I asked Pete. "Are the Baileys digging a bomb shelter? Their yard looks like a Korean War zone. What about a pool? Are the Bailey brothers getting a swimming pool? With their own pool, they won't have to worry about getting polio from the public swimming pool."

"Maybe they're fixing an underground sewer pipe that sprang a leak," said Pete.

I wrinkled my nose. "We called Squirt-Not Sewer Service when ours leaked."

Just then the Bailey brothers ran out of their gate like twin tornadoes. Pete left us to follow them around the corner onto the street called The Wye. We stayed with Mary Jane. Cherrylee Elementary School sat on a tree-filled lot at the end of the street. There The Wye split into two different streets that curved around the school like a horseshoe. Crowds of kids streamed into Cherrylee's tan-colored, Art Deco buildings.

"Hey, Carol Ann," a chorus sounded behind me. Two of my good friends rushed to catch me. Tall, blonde Susan and short, brunette Becky reached my side. They sputtered and gulped for breath. In front of us, I watched Ernie's '32 roar past our school.

"We ran...as fast...as we...could...to catch up with you," gasped Becky.

"You walk...too fast," puffed Susan. "I like your cute blouse. Is it new?"

"Thanks and, yes, it is new," I said as I fingered the pearl buttons on my white blouse. "Girls, guess what our neighbor, Mr. Chester, has in his backyard?"

"Isn't he your mean neighbor with a yard full of chickens?" asked Becky.

"He is, but his cute puppy escaped into my yard the other day," I said.

"What kind of puppy?" asked Susan as she kept walking.

"Pete says he's a Beagle puppy," I said. "He's about 8 inches tall and real cute. He likes to hide from Mr. Chester under the bushes by the fence." I sighed.

We followed the boys and giggling girls through the schoolyard. Our fifth grade classroom bustled with activity. I liked the colorful bulletin boards decorated with springtime bunnies, birds, and flowers. We only had a few more days until Easter.

Riiiiiiiiiiiiiiiiiiiiiiiiiiiiiiiiiiing.

Everyone scrambled for their seats. My nice friend, Lois, sat in the desk next to me. I smoothed my skirt then folded my hands on the desktop. Luckily, I sat at my own desk. Some lower grade pupils had to share desks in overcrowded classrooms.

On the chalkboard behind our teacher's desk, chalked lettering spelled out the date, "Wednesday, April 6, 1955," and our assignments. A red March of Dimes can sat on Miss Nelson's desk. When that can is filled up with dimes, it will help find a cure for polio. Mom said an actor named Eddie Cantor told Americans to give their dimes so those dimes could march all the way to the White House. That's how the March of Dimes started.

"Good morning, class," said Miss Nelson. She began taking attendance. She called out forty-two names and heard "here" forty-one times.

Because Miss Nelson wore glasses, the boys called her Miss Four Eyes. *Did she buy her glasses at Dr. D. Silver's office downtown?* Miss Nelson stood up. She wore a smart-looking navy suit. "Flag Salute Leader, please step forward," said Miss Nelson.

Lois walked to the front of the class. She stood facing the beautiful American flag proudly hanging on a flagpole in the corner. Red, white, and blue symbolized our nation. Lois said, "Please stand and place your hand over your heart."

We stood at attention and proudly recited the pledge to our flag. "I pledge allegiance to the Flag of the United States of America and to the Republic for which it stands, one Nation under God, indivisible, with liberty and justice for all."

"Thank you, Lois. You may sit down. Did anyone read the *El Monte Herald*, so they can share a current event with the class?" asked Miss Nelson.

Carolyn raised her hand. "I did." She read, "Fire hydrant mowed down. A city fire hydrant was the victim of a hit-and-run case in El Monte early Monday morning."

Shary raised her hand and read, "$302 worth of cash, jewelry taken by thief."

"Thrifty Drug features new fishing offer," offered Laura.

I raised my hand and nervously read my article from the

El Monte Herald. "Special training course offered in Civil Defense Medical Health Service. Tonight will mark the opening session of a training course for physicians in Area D, Region 9, Civil Defense, according to announcement." *Are we in danger in Area D, Region 9?*

Pete read a baseball article. "High-riding Aztecs will play host to second-place Lions. The scene is set for a big high school fray on Friday, April 15, when the league-leading Aztecs match base hits with the second-place El Monte Lions on the Aztec field."

"Go, Lions, go!" Lawrence stood and yelled. "Oops. Sorry for the interruption," said Lawrence as he sat down.

"Please raise your hand next time, Lawrence," said Miss Nelson.

Christina ended our current events with a very scary article. She read, "Seventy-six percent of second graders to get vaccine. The vaccine which has been under study for a full year is hoped by medical authorities to prevent polio."

Yikes. Even our newspaper is talking about the polio vaccine.

A classroom-wide whisper escaped into the air. Miss Nelson raised her hand for silence. "Thank you for sharing those interesting and informative current events."

I pulled my arithmetic book and homework from my desk. Arithmetic topped the list as my toughest subject. I turned to page 203. Aunt Ruthie had lots of tough subjects when she attended schools in Chicago. She studied her subjects by kerosene lantern when their electricity got turned off, because they were so poor. Her mother, Granny Mary, and her three brothers were on Relief, which was government money in the 1930s.

Like a classic car cruising Main Street, I drove through my

subjects for the morning: Arithmetic, Reading, Social Studies, Science, Spelling, and finally Hygiene.

Riiiiiiiiiiiiiiiiiiiiiiiiiiiiiiiiiiiiiiiiiiiiiiiiiiiiig.

Lunch time at last! My stomach growled. Delicious food smells drifted through the open door. Today the cafetorium served mashed potatoes with hamburger gravy, green beans, and chocolate cake. *Lucky Pete,* I thought. *He gets to buy lunch today. I get to eat a peanut butter sandwich, chips, and a cookie from my lunch pail.*

The Cherrylee cafetorium beat like the heart of our school. The office and classrooms, with their outside halls, formed a protective hug around the school grounds. That's what Mom liked to say about Cherrylee School. *I wish I could put a protective hug around Hey Pup right now. Would Dad talk to Mr. Chester about buying Hey Pup if I asked him?*

Last month, on Open House night, I brought Dad to school. I proudly showed him off to all my friends. Tall, dark, and handsome described my dad, Harry Hartnell. That night, even Becky said, "Your dad looks like a movie star."

Today at the drinking fountain I leaned over to get a drink, or "suck the stream," as Pete would say. The cool water wet my dry mouth and throat. I looked down. A big blob of pink, already-chewed, bubble gum oozed in a gooey glob next to the drain. *Yuck.* I left the fountain.

Inside the cafetorium, school children screeched like wild animals. Pupils fidgeted in the lunch line, swung lunch pails, raced for chairs, wiggled in their chairs, and climbed on top of chairs! The noise grew until a teacher blew her whistle. I looked up at the uniquely carved rafters near the ceiling. I expected to see swinging monkeys. This zoo needed some cages. Pete and his wild friends would be first in line for them.

After lunch, Pete ran outside with the Bailey boys. *Did he ask about their dirt piles? Are they digging a fallout shelter? Will steps drop down into a deep, dark scary hole? Will it save the Baileys from an atom bomb? Should my family dig a dark, safe fallout shelter, too?* I followed my friends outside into the sunlight and stopped thinking about fallout shelters.

The playground swarmed like a beehive. Students played foursquare, tetherball, hopscotch, and jump rope. Groups of kids kneeled in the dirt to flick their marbles around. I liked playing marbles, but I hated getting dirty. I really hated losing my favorite marbles. I loved my cats-eyes and clearies the best, so I kept them in a pink leather bag.

"Let's jump rope," said my friend, Eileen.

"I'll hold the other end of it," I said.

She loosened the jump rope and then swooshed it around. I grabbed one end of it and stood across from her. Over and over and over we whipped that rope. I wanted to forget the scary current events this morning. *Isn't anyone else worried?* Susan and Becky took turns jumping in and out of the jump rope like nothing was wrong.

"Let's give them red-hot chili peppers," I said to Eileen. We whipped that rope into a blur. Then they took the rope and turned it while we jumped inside of its circle.

Breathless, hot, and tired, we retreated to our classroom for a rest and the remainder of our subjects. Handwriting, Art, and Physical Education finished our school day. At exactly 2:20 P.M., Miss Nelson reminded us about our homework and a class party the next day. The class quieted when Miss Nelson mentioned the "party" word.

"Remember, students, all your homework must be turned in tomorrow before our Easter party. Lois's mother has offered to bring refreshments. This Friday, April 8, is Good Friday. You're out of school. Have fun during your Easter Break next week, but remember to bring your dimes for the March of Dimes Drive after the break. Also, please keep in mind your assignment that's due on Tuesday, April 19. Class dismissed."

As I gathered my books, I wanted to dismiss Christina's current event from my mind. The words she read said that a lot of second graders were getting a polio vaccine. I hoped our Cherrylee second graders wouldn't be lined up someday soon for a scary shot of vaccine. If they were, they would need courage.

What is that Bible verse in Deuteronomy about bravery? How does it go? Oh, yeah, it says, "Be strong and of good courage." Could I be strong and of good courage when it was my turn to get a polio vaccine? Could I have Pete's kind of courage?

Chapter Five

The Mud Hole

▼▼▼▼▼▼▼▼▼▼▼▼▼▼▼▼▼▼▼

Yippee! No homework for a week! Easter Break has officially started! I thought with excitement. Our class Easter party ended the school day. I happily carried jellybeans and a chocolate bunny in my bag. Pete walked next to me on The Wye. We passed the pink house with the funny-looking fence. A long time ago, someone shaped the white iron bars of the fence, so they looked like white-iron, peacock tail feathers. When we got to La Madera Avenue, we turned toward home. Once there, we could check on Hey Pup.

"Did you ever ask the Baileys why they're digging up their yard?" I asked Pete.

"Yeah, they're digging a big hole," he answered. "That hole seems like it's really boss, you know, it's really great."

"But *why* are they digging a big, boss hole?" I asked.

"Ask them yourself, Miss Nosey. Here they come," Pete said, pointing.

But those Bailey brothers blurred past us before I got the chance. They disappeared into their yard. Pete and I followed. *What's hiding behind those dirt piles? I sniffed. Sniff, sniff, sniff. I don't smell anything stinky. Their sewer must be okay. Are they getting a pool filled with clean, polio-free water? Then we wouldn't have to be afraid to play in the pool. When will the heavy equipment roll into their yard? If they aren't getting a pool, could they be digging a fallout shelter?*

"What are you boys digging over there?" I asked. "Can we see it? Is it a swimming pool? Are you getting the ground ready for the big digging machine?"

They laughed then waved us further into the yard with their shovels.

"This isn't a swimming pool," the older brother said. "We're digging a big, round hole with an island in the middle."

"We're digging a moat," said the younger boy as he kept digging.

What a disappointment. "What fun can you have in a muddy moat?" I asked.

"Let's look at it, Carol Ann," said Pete as he bravely walked next to a dirt mound.

I followed carefully. "I'll look at the moat if I don't get dirty," I said.

The huge, donut-shaped hole measured about 10-feet by 10-feet with a round island in the middle. *Is a moat like a fallout shelter? Where is the roof?* Dirt piles lay everywhere. Grass chunks littered each dirt mound like tufts of green hair.

"Did you boys get permission to dig up your yard for a moat type fallout shelter?" I asked them as I looked around. "You could use a fallout shelter now that your yard looks like a Korean War zone."

The younger brother stopped digging. He said, "Before our dad went out of town for a few days, we asked him if we could dig a hole in the yard. Dad said, 'Okay.' By the way, a moat isn't a fallout shelter."

Pete started laughing. "Yeah, Carol Ann. A moat is a ditch around a castle, filled up with water, to keep out their enemies," he said. "My dad would be my enemy if I dug a ditch like this one in our yard. But...since it's your yard, how can I help?"

"Go get the water hose. Drag it over here," said Bob Bailey.

"Pete, I think it's time to leave. Let's go," I said. Normally, when school got out, we walked straight home. This looked too messy. Those brothers stood knee deep in that hole. They climbed out to help Pete drag the hose over to it. The hose lay twisted on the grass like a long green snake.

"Let her rip," a boy's voice yelled. The green hose came to life. Water sprayed out in waves. Pete grabbed the hose back to earth. He plunged the hose nozzle into the moat. Muddy water rose up like Noah's flood.

Those crazy boys jumped around hollering, "Like wow...unreal...boss." Muddy water splashed everywhere.

They kneeled down. I couldn't see what they were doing. I dropped my school bag to walk closer. Several boats floated around. The hose pumped water into the hole. The water made a swirling, foaming, muddy mess. The three boys took off their shoes and socks then climbed into the mud hole. Pete pushed a boat on the dirty water. The Bailey boys placed play soldiers on the edge then dove the soldiers into the water.

"This is great!" Pete yelled. "Get over here and get in, Carol Ann. Get with it."

"I don't want to get with it," I said as I stood there watching in disgust. "Aren't you afraid of getting polio from playing in muddy water?"

"Naaah," said Pete as he continued with their fun.

I hated getting dirty, but temptation tugged at me, "Miss Nosey." *If I take my shoes and socks off, I can touch the water with my toes. That way, only my toes will get dirty.* I sat down on the edge of the donut-shaped hole. I scooped up the muddy water with my hand and let it cascade from my fingers. Fools' gold sparkled in the ripples.

If I got into the mud hole very carefully and held up my plaid skirt, I wouldn't get my skirt wet. I slipped slowly into the mud hole. The cool water swirled around my knees in that funny brown pool/moat/mud hole. Suddenly, a car door slammed nearby.

"What's going on?" A mad male voice yelled, "My yard...my beautiful yard! What have you boys done to it?"

I turned around to see who yelled so loudly. *Oh no, I'm losing my balance!* I fell down! I stood up sputtering. Muddy water cascaded from me in waves. *Yikes. I'm in trouble now.* A dreadful dirt taste filled my mouth. My teeth gritted together. I looked down at my clothes. Brown mud stained my white sweater and blouse. I looked like a chocolate bunny.

"OUT!" An angry voice screamed. "O...U...T. OUT!"

Pete and I did just that. We jumped out of the mud hole, grabbed our stuff, and cut out. Like two barefooted rockets, we blasted down the street. Our drag racing abilities would leave Ernie's '32 in the dust. I glanced at Pete's muddy new look. His mom might not be too mad, but my dirty outfit spelled trouble with a capital T! I always wanted a brown sweater, now I had one. My plaid soggy skirt stuck to my legs. *Yuck.*

Pete called to me, "Carol Ann, you look grody...you're all covered in mud."

As we ran, I kept looking back. "At least...no one...is chasing after us," I gasped.

We stopped at Pete's driveway near Hawk's hot rod and the teenagers. From the porch, Mary Jane spotted us and yelled, "Mom! You have to see this!" Out of her wide-open mouth she asked us, "What happened? Did you two go swimming in a mud hole?"

"Sort of," Pete answered. Then he turned to me and said, "I'm sorry, Carol Ann. You're a muddy mess. It's my fault that I didn't listen to you. Wow, Mr. Bailey went ape over his dug-up yard. When I looked back, he was chasing his boys with a thick, black belt. They ran in circles around the mud hole."

"Mr. Bailey's temper boiled over," I said. "I didn't know a person's face could get so red! It looked like a firecracker ready to explode!"

Hawk motioned us over. "Did you seriously go swimming in a mud hole?"

Pete said, "We didn't go swimming in it. I walked in it and Carol Ann fell in it."

Ernie laughed as he dumped some tools next to Hawk's hot rod. Tim smiled really big then awkwardly sat down on a crate next to the car. He leaned his crutches near him. Metal braces, peeking out of the bottom of his jeans, helped Tim to bend his legs. I didn't want to stare, so I looked down at my muddy sleeves and shook them.

Tim said, "Hey, Hawk, remember the time I fell in a mud hole when I first started walking around with my crutches? It happened last year when I'd just gotten out of Sister Kenny's Polio Hospital. Even though I had two years of rehabilitation,

I still couldn't walk very well. It was raining like crazy that day when your dad pulled into Dan's Diner. I got out of your dad's car, balanced on my crutches, and *BAM*, down I went into the mud."

Hawk laughed as he shook his head up and down. "Yeah, I had to help you up. You looked as muddy as these kids. You looked like you went swimming in a mud hole."

We all laughed at that. Then Pete asked, "Hey, Tim, how old were you when you got polio? Could you still go to school?"

Tim said, "I got polio three years ago when I was 13. My mom thought I just had a bad cold. When I couldn't walk, I got rushed to the polio hospital. I lived there for two years while I had daily therapy. I worked on school work when I could."

Pete said, "I bet you'll be able to walk without your crutches someday."

Tim smiled and said, "I hope so kid. I sure hope so." Hawk patted Tim on the back then walked towards us. He stood there smiling and shaking his head.

Yelp, woof, woof. Something barked behind me. I turned around and watched Hey Pup crawl under our gate. He popped up into Pete's yard and ran towards me. He stood up against my muddy leg. Then he casually walked over and sniffed Tim's crutches with the big black nose on his tan and white face. His tail wagged wildly. Tim scooped him up and got his face licked.

Tim scrunched up his freshly licked face and asked, "Who owns this baby hound dog? His breed is great at hunting. Beagles love to chase things. They're built to run...like Hawk's Ride. He'll run for miles someday. He's a great family dog, too."

"He belongs to my neighbor, Mr. Chester," I said.

Pete explained, "Old Mr. Chester yells 'hey pup' when he's looking for this little guy."

I held out my mud-soaked sleeves and said, "I can take him." *He's such a cutie.*

Pete answered, "Aw, gee, Carol Ann, let the pup hang out here. Tim wants a clean face. The pup can run around here for a while with us. We'll watch out for him. Before dark, I'll bring him back through your yard and slip him under Mr. C's fence. You'd better go home. You're shaking like crazy in your wet, muddy clothes."

I nodded my head and with chattering teeth said, "Bring Hey Pup back when he's done licking everyone." I pointed to myself. "Miss Nosey found out about those dirt piles and the messy mud hole all right." My chocolate-colored sweater sleeves shook in a shiver. I half-smiled at Pete then waved goodbye, slinging mud blobs into the air.

My smile faded as I walked through our yard. Even the laundry mocked me. Dad's very white shirt fluttered in the breeze. It pointed an arm in my direction. Mom's clean, red-checkered apron waved accusing ties at me. Even the dish-towels angrily snapped their hems. Kathleen, Gail, and the cousins were playing on the swings.

In a way, I wish the Baileys did dig a fallout shelter instead of a dumb moat. Their fallout shelter could protect us from a nuclear strike. It could protect Hey Pup and even mean old Mr. Chester. Driving to a downtown shelter would take too long. *Could we dig a fallout shelter in our yard?* I'd ask Dad about it. A muddy drip rolled down my nose. I wiped my face and shivered some more. Having our own fallout shelter would help me to be brave...like Tim.

O God, help me please, I prayed. *Please give Mom some extra patience, so she won't be too mad about my muddy clothes.* I walked quickly by the swing set. The kids stopped swinging. They stared at me as I shivered again. Then I shook my muddy sleeves one more time. No more mud holes for me.

"What happened to you, Carol Ann?" Gail asked as she jumped off her swing. "You're all muddy. Did you fall in the gutter?" she asked me. "I hope you don't get polio from muddy gutter water! I hope you don't get polio like Hawk's friend, Tim!"

I slowly walked into the house and heard, "CAROL ANN HARTNELL!"

Chapter Six

Mr. Chester

▼▲▼▲▼▲▼▲▼▲▼▲▼▲▼▲▼▲▼▲▼▲▼▲

Mighty Mouse flew to the rescue inside our old black and white television set. Dad didn't let us watch the color television set without him or Mom. Light flickered on my sisters' faces. Pete punched at the air. We loved watching cartoons with Pete. Sometimes it seemed like he lived at our house. He only went home when he had to.

We laughed loudly as Mighty Mouse swooped down then dodged Harry the cat. "Here I am to save the day," he sang out loud. "That means that Mighty Mouse is on the way." The bad cartoon characters ran around causing all kinds of trouble for Mighty Mouse. As the hero, he worked hard to help the good cartoon characters. We liked that.

Earlier, I washed the breakfast dishes and put them away. Then Kathleen and I swept the kitchen, made our beds, straightened up our bedroom, and got dressed for the day. Even baby Mark, the wiggle-worm, was dressed for a while.

He'd stay in his clothes until gooey baby food dropped on them. Doing our chores took all morning.

Pete licked his lips. He said, "Your mom makes boss waffles. They're great. I smothered mine in butter and maple syrup. Mmmmm…m."

"I did, too," I said, "and now I'm stuffed. My shorts feel tight." I looked down at my red shorts and striped cotton top. My white tennis shoes and socks looked clean and neat. I'd try to keep them that way. I didn't want a repeat of the mud hole incident. Mom scolded me about turning my white sweater into a brown blob. My punishment was to buy a new sweater with my allowance and fold laundry for a month.

I looked at Pete. His flickering face was smiling at Mighty Mouse's new dilemma. He clapped as Mighty Mouse saved Pearl Pureheart from Harry the villainous cat. *I wish Mighty Mouse could save Hey Pup from villainous Mr. Chester.* Pete's bouncing shook our old, gray, hide-a-bed sofa. I felt the scratchy sofa fabric on my legs.

"What are you youngsters watching?" Mary Jane asked from the doorway. Using her superior voice she said, "It sounds like cartoons."

I popped up from our old sofa in embarrassment. "We're helping my sisters find a channel," I lied. "They like to watch *Mighty Mouse* in the morning."

"It looks like you kiddies are watching that channel. You're too old for cartoons," she mocked.

"Who let you in, Mary Jane?" asked Pete. "What do you want?"

"Mrs. Hartnell let me in," Mary Jane said with a smirk. "I'm bored, so Mom said to find you or wash the kitchen floor. I'm here so let's *do* something."

Pete heaved a sigh. "Can't you go talk to Hawk and his friends?"

"No," she said. "They're leaving. I'm not allowed to ride in Ernie's hot rod. Mom said Ernie needs to slow down or Hawk won't be riding with him either."

Pete said, "Okay, let's go, Carol Ann. Let's go do…something."

The screen door slammed behind us as we followed Mary Jane outside. My bangs fluttered in the warm air. A rose-perfumed breeze drifted under my nose along with a stinky smell from Mr. Chester's yard. Chirping birds chattered in the trees and competed with the rock and roll tunes from Hawk's radio next door.

Mary Jane snickered as she asked, "Why are your Easter baskets sitting out in your living room? Do you think the Easter Bunny will fill them up?"

"My sisters and brother think he will," I answered. "We always put our Easter baskets out, so the Bunny can fill them with candy and goodies. Don't you?"

Pete said, "Our baskets magically appear on Easter morning filled with jelly bird eggs, candy-coated marshmallow eggs, and big chocolate rabbits." He licked his lips in anticipation. "Even Hawk gets a basket from the Bunny."

"Why, Peter James Hawking, I think you still believe in the Easter Bunny," Mary Jane laughed. "Why aren't you hunting colored eggs at Lambert Park this morning? Mom took Mandy over to the park, so she could hunt eggs."

"Aw, knock it off, sis," Pete said. "Why do you bother us if you think we're babies? You'd have fun hunting eggs at Lambert Park. Dad said they hid 3,000 of them."

"I'm bored, not crazy," said Mary Jane. "That park is

crawling with kids. No thanks. What are you doing besides watching cartoons? Can you do something fun and clean? I don't want to get dirty like you did the other day in that mud hole. Walking home, covered in mud, is not my idea of fun. Can we see Mr. Chester's puppy?"

She smoothed her hands down the front of her white shorts. Embroidered daisies decorated her white, sleeveless blouse. Pink socks peeked out of white tennis shoes.

Peep. Peep. Peep. Baby chicks ran across the backyard grass. They looked like yellow fuzz balls with twig legs. A squawking white hen and a barking puppy followed them past us as we stood still to stare. The pup stopped, lifted his head, and howled.

Awhooooooo! Squawk. Cluck. Cluck. Squawk. Woof. Woof.

"Oh, how cute," said Mary Jane. "You have baby chicks and a puppy for Easter. The chicks look like they ran out of a picture postcard. Can I have one?"

"They don't belong to us," I told her. "They live here in our chicken car, but they belong to Mr. Chester." I pointed to the back fence. "Hey Pup belongs to him, too." I looked down. "Hi, baby hound dog. Mr. Chester won't want you to chase his chickens."

"Mr. Chester's mean. I'm glad he doesn't live behind us," Mary Jane said.

"Yeah," said Pete. "He's an oddball. He's got a chicken farm back there. His birds cut out into Carol Ann's yard all the time. His watch dogs growl and bark a lot."

Mary Jane walked into our backyard. "If I ask him nicely, maybe he'll let me have one of his chicks," she said. "He might even give me *two* chicks."

Mary Jane stopped in front of our bush-covered fence. A

space, with a view, opened up in the middle of the bushes when Mary Jane pushed and pulled at the branches. The three-by-three opening revealed old chain-link fencing and Mr. Chester's two-acre yard. We stood next to her and eye-balled his place. Hey Pup sniffed a rock.

Giant walnut trees cast shadows on a dirt patch bordered in grass. A big tree stump poked out of the ground in the middle of the dirt. Rusty brown stains covered the stump. Two-dozen red chickens, plus a few white ones, scratched at the ground.

Cluck. Cluck. Cluck.

Further back on Mr. Chester's lot, another chain-link fence stretched across the yard in front of some wooden build-ings. A concrete sidewalk bisected the grass then slipped under the closed gate. Two mangy-looking dogs ran up to the gate. They barked at us across the yard. We ducked down to hide behind the shrubbery. Hey Pup sat down next to me. I scratched his droopy ears and head.

Mary Jane pushed at the branches again. She made a peep-hole under the larger opening to get the best view. Pete and I moved sideways to make our own peepholes. I looked at the whole yard from my spot. Stinky smells came from the yard, so I pinched my nose. Mary Jane pinched her nose, too. The pup sniffed. *Sniff, sniff, sniff.*

Pete looked at us. He laughed. "You smell chicken poop," he said. "That smell is raunchy and real stinky, but you'll get used to it." Pete tickled the puppy's chin.

"I don't think I'll ever get used to that smell," I said with a funny voice because of my pinched nostrils. "I smell it all the time. I'm not used to it yet." The puppy wrinkled his nose in agreement.

"Mr. Chester's got a boss chicken business back there," Pete said. "All those buildings are hen houses. He's got a larger operation than my grandpa Peter."

"Grandpa's yard isn't as big," volunteered Mary Jane, also in a pinched voice. She looked down at the puppy and said, "Our grandpa has a dog just like that one. He's cute."

Hey Pup thumped his tail on my red shorts. "Pete," I asked, "is that how you know about the hen houses? Do you help your grandpa take care of his chickens?"

"Yep, Grandpa lets me and Hawk work to gather eggs. He pays us, too. Grandpa's hen houses have rows of nests and perches, plus a board walkway with wire-mesh below it. A ton of chicken droppings fall on the ground. You smell chicken droppings."

I nodded my head up and down. "Chicken stuff stinks."

"I bet Mr. Chester owns hundreds of White-Leggers. They lay lots of eggs for Easter." said Pete. "Did you know chickens need 12 hours of sunlight every day?"

Mary Jane said, "Mom bought a bunch of eggs to boil. Kids all over town dyed tons of eggs for Easter egg hunts today. Right now, Mandy's running around the park searching for dyed eggs. I would only pick up pink eggs if I was hunting."

"Gee, Pete, you know a bunch about chickens," I squeaked. Hey Pup looked up.

"My gramps tells me all about chickens," said Pete. "When I go to Grandpa's house, he lets me feed his chickens."

"I bet it's a tough job to feed chickens and take care of them," I said.

"Twice a day, they get scratch feed made of oats and cracked corn," said Pete. "Plus, they get mash made from oats, cracked corn, barley, and other stuff. Look at those Rhode Island Reds. They're scratching for feed. Chickens also need grit, grass or lawn clippings, and lots of fresh water. And they don't like a little hound dog barking at them."

"Where are the baby chicks?" Mary Jane asked.

"They're over in those warm brooder houses," Pete answered his sister.

"Mary Jane, don't you ever help your grandpa with his chickens?" I asked.

"Never," she answered. "That kind of work is too dirty and stinky."

"I think we've seen enough, Pete," I said as I nudged him. I patted Hey Pup again. Squatting down in the dirt cramped my legs. A scratch on my arm oozed blood. *Ouch. I scratched my arm on something. Yikes. I don't want a Tetanus shot just because I got scratched by these bushes covered in rust spots. What are these spots, anyway?*

"Wait a minute, Carol Ann," Pete said. He pushed his peephole even wider. Scratchy, dusty bushes didn't bother Pete. "We can't split yet. He'll hear us leave."

Woof. Woof. Woof. Yelp. Yelp. Hey Pup sat up and sniffed at the fence.

A barking dog dashed away from the black boot that kicked it. The owner of the boot stood at the gate. It was Mr. Chester! The old man looked like bad news and big trouble.

Yikes. "Let's go, Pete," I begged. "Mr. Chester will see us with his puppy."

"*Shhhh,* Carol Ann, it's too late now," Pete whispered. "Cool it and hide the pup. We'll slip him back under the fence when Mr. Chester goes back to his house."

"He might walk over this way looking for Hey Pup," I said. "I'm scared."

Mary Jane scrunched down closer to the ground. Dirt spots smudged her white shorts. Leaves rested in her curly, blonde hair like a green halo. Her dirty fingers still pinched her nose. Brown stripes streaked her cheeks. She'd flip if she looked in a mirror.

"Be here at 6:00 A.M. and no later," snapped Mr. Chester. Hey Pup lifted his ear.

"Sure thing, Boss," a voice answered in the distance.

The gate creaked open. "Get outa my way, you mangy mongrels," he said. "Good fer nothing dogs. Where'd that pesky pup disappear to again? What a mistake to let my daughter drop him off here," mumbled Mr. Chester angrily. "Let me get some dinner."

He limped toward us on the sidewalk. Up and down stomped his black boots covered in globs of goop. Spots and stains dotted his dirty denim overalls. Crumpled pants disguised crippled legs of different lengths. A swollen, speckled hand gripped a creepy crutch. The crutch was tucked into his armpit, under his misshapen shoulder. Mr. Chester's crooked body leaned like a broken branch.

Coarse whiskers covered the wrinkled, tanned skin on his blotchy face. Gray, frizzled hair stood up on his head like Granny Mary's mop. He spit out a long, brown stream of something. *Yuck.* The puppy started shaking, so I pulled him onto my lap.

Mr. Chester looked crippled, crotchety, and crazy. An overpowering sweat-smell punished the air when I unpinched my nose. Then I noticed *his* nose. Horrible, gruesome gray hairs curled out of both nostrils on his nose. Sad-looking, sinister Mr. Chester turned. He slowly shuffled away. Hey Pup whimpered and snuggled closer to me.

Pete leaned toward me. He whispered, "Does poor Mr. Chester have tusks growing out of his nose?"

In that moment, I felt sorry for Mr. Chester and the kid he used to be. He probably never had a good friend like Pete. Because of his crippled legs, he probably never rode a bike, or played hopscotch, or jumped rope, or ran in the grass, or hid in the bushes on a warm day to spy on someone. He probably struggled through every step in his life. Our fun adventure didn't feel fun anymore. My heart hurt for old Mr. Chester. I didn't care if Pete called me a party-pooper.

"Oh, Pete, we're so mean to spy on Mr. Chester. We're meaner than he is," I moaned softly. Hey Pup licked my hand.

"I know, Carol Ann. I'm sorry we stayed too long," said Pete.

"Well, I'm not sorry we're here. I still want a baby chick," Mary Jane said loudly. She blew a giant pink bubble gum bubble. *Pop.* Pink gum blanketed her nose. She scraped the dirty pink gum off her nose and shoved it back into her mouth. *Yuck.*

"Be quiet, stop blowing bubbles, and quit moving around, Mary Jane," Pete whispered. "You're shaking the bushes. He'll see us."

Mr. Chester stopped on the sidewalk. He looked right at me through my peephole. He squinted at me with cloudy, brown eyes. I ducked down. I kneeled in the dirt next to the puppy. Maybe he didn't see us after all.

"I might be crippled, but I'm not blind. I can hear real good, too," mumbled Mr. Chester as he limped off the sidewalk. His crutch crumpled the grass with each step. The chickens scattered everywhere. A red hen flew onto the fence. Hey Pup scrambled up, stood with his legs against the fence, and *woofed* at her.

"Be quiet puppy. Mr. Chester will hear you and find us," I whispered.

"Get back here, you red devil," Mr. Chester yelled at the chicken on top of the fence. With feathers flying, the scared chicken dropped behind me then ran across our yard. Several soft feathers floated onto my lap. "I'll show 'em," grumbled Mr. Chester.

Yikes. Will he show us or the chickens? I wondered. Be *brave.* I picked up Hey Pup and held him close to me. He *woofed, sniffed,* and shook in my shaking arms. *Would mean old Mr. Chester hurt him?*

Squawk. Squawk. Squawk.

Pete whispered in awe, "For a crooked old guy, he's got a lightening-fast arm. He grabbed that chicken while I blinked."

"What's he gonna do to it?" I whispered. Hey Pup whimpered.

Mary Jane stood up in the opening so she could see the commotion. I turned back to my peephole.

"Carol Ann, you might want to close your eyes." Pete's warning was too late.

TH…WACK!

Mr. Chester's axe stuck in the stump. A red-feathered chicken body ran in our direction. Blood sprayed on the bushes. Hey Pup snuggled in my arms to hide.

"What a horrible thing to do," squealed Mary Jane. She stood there like a statue. "What a horrible, hateful, old man."

Mr. Chester walked up to the fence. He shook his fist in a menacing manner. "I saw your sneaky spy-eyes staring at me through the fence," he said. "My business is none of your business. I ought to call your folks. Send my pup back under the fence. He don't belong in your yard."

I put Hey Pup down on the ground so he could go home. He cocked his head to one side like he understood his master's mean words. Then he put his face down on his paws.

I stood up tall like my hero, John Wayne. He always did the right thing and I would, too. *O God, help me please,* I prayed. *Help me to be brave. Give me courage, because I'm afraid.* With a shaky voice I said, "You're right, Mr. Chester. We're sorry for spying on you. We're sorry for snooping into your business."

He shrugged, turned around, picked up his dinner from the ground, and limped away. Hey Pup scooted under the bush-covered fence and ran after his grizzled, old owner. Mr. Chester limped through his gate and slammed it shut behind him and the pup.

Pete and I stood there stunned. Red spots covered Pete's face and clothes. I looked down at my clothes. My red shorts hid most of the blood, but measle-like spots dotted my arms, legs, and striped top. I had my answer about the mysterious rust spots.

"Yikes, Pete, you're covered in blood spots," I said. He wiped his spotty face with his T-shirt. Then he wiped his spotty hands on his spotty blue jeans.

Pete asked, "Where's Mighty Mouse to save the day when we need him? We poked our noses where they didn't belong and we got 'shot down.' Poor, old, mean Mr. Chester really went ape. He scolded us royally. I hope Hey Pup will be okay."

"That Mr. Chester is a horrible, mean, nasty, crippled, crusty old man. I hope he chokes on his chicken dinner," yelled Mary Jane. "Look at me. I'm a mess!"

We looked at her, and normally perfect Mary Jane *was* a

mess. Blood spots sprinkled her from curls to shoes. Red dots spotted her white shorts and shared space on her embroidered daisy blouse. Mary Jane looked down at her blood-smeared hands and started screaming, shouting, and running.

Pete said, "All you need is a little soap and water, sis. Cool it."

"I'm telling Mom on you, Peter James Hawking! This is *your* fault," she cried as she ran around the corner of my house.

"Don't have a cow, Mary Jane," Pete called after her. Turning back to me he said, "She's real upset. At this point, Mary Jane's wishing she ran home dripping in mud instead of…the other stuff. Hunting Easter eggs at the park would have been safer and a lot cleaner. At least she didn't get bored being around us."

"We're never boring," I said, "and we gave her something to do." We giggled.

"Carol Ann, you were really brave when you talked to Mr. Chester and told him we were sorry. You swooped in just like Mighty Mouse to save the day. You had a lot of courage."

Heat flooded my face. "The Bible says to love thy neighbor. Spying on Mr. Chester was unloving. That's why I said, 'sorry,' even though he scared me shaky. Poor Hey Pup was scared shaky, too. I didn't feel very courageous, but thanks for saying it."

We walked in our red-spattered clothes to my front door. Pete asked, "What're you doing later?"

"If I'm not in too much trouble, I'm dying Easter eggs while I watch John Wayne and Andy Devine in the *Stagecoach* movie," I said. "John Wayne is my hero, and he's so courageous in this movie. He's very handsome, too."

"Wow, I dig *Stagecoach* and how the cowboys get chased

by Native American Indians. Arrows fly everywhere," said Pete. He looked at me, then down at his clothes. "Just like in the movie, we look like the victims of a bloody massacre. Even Hey Pup got sprinkled. He looked like a Beagle/Dalmatian mix with red spots instead of black."

My cousin, Little Charlie, walked up to us. He stared at us with bulging eyes. "Did you have a car accident in Ernie's hot rod? You're all bloody."

"No, we didn't have a hot rod accident," I said. "We got too close to Mr. Chester and a chicken accident." I brushed at my blood stained arms.

"I hope you can't get polio from chicken blood," Gail wailed when she saw us.

From inside the house Kathleen opened the screen door, looked at us in surprise, and yelled, "Mom, get out here quick! Pete and Carol Ann had an accident in Ernie's hot rod! They're bleeding to death!"

Chapter Seven

Easter

▀▄▀▄▀▄▀▄▀▄▀▄▀▄▀▄▀▄▀▄▀▄▀▄▀▄

Easter morning sparkled like a diamond in bright sunlight. My heart fluttered excitedly. First thing today we'd walk to church, attend Bible class, and then go to the Easter morning service. Afterwards, we'd try to stand still for family photos, hunt Easter eggs, eat Easter candy, and enjoy the food buffet. Pete called it the "buffet bash." Then we'd take more pictures, eat more candy, and run around with our cousins.

Ruffled petticoats swished under my beautiful aqua-blue Easter dress. I loved the lace overlay on my skirt that swayed back and forth with each step. I touched the lacy collar that framed my face.

I clutched a white, vinyl purse with my white-gloved hands. Treasures rattled in my purse: some jellybeans, my church offering, and an Easter card with two dollars from Granny Catherine and Great-Aunt Julie who lived in Chicago, Illinois. A thin, white sweater draped over my arm. What a special day.

Pete called Easter "the most"…a great day filled with lots of goodies. *I wonder what goodies Pete got in his Easter basket. Did Hey Pup get any puppy treats?* Goodies filled my Easter basket up to its brim. Colorful jelly gum eggs, nougat eggs, a chocolate bunny, and a candy-filled plastic bunny nestled in my basket's fake green grass.

"Wait for us, Carol Ann," Kathleen called.

I turned around to see Kathleen and Gail. They looked like spring flowers in their Easter dresses. Kathleen wore a blue floral dress. Gail looked adorable in yellow chiffon. A breeze tugged at our Easter hats. Mr. Chester's yucky yard smells faded under the sweet smells of honeysuckle and roses. *Poor Hey Pup has to sniff yucky smells everyday.*

Gail shook her purse. "Carol Ann, Mommy gave me money for the offerry." She shook her purse again, loving the sound.

"You mean the offering, Gail," I corrected. "That's when we give our money to help the church pay its bills and stuff."

"I've got my offering, too," said Kathleen.

"Remember to put your offering in the plate that gets passed around during the church service," I said. My sisters nodded their heads up and down.

Aunt Ruthie waited for us on the driveway. "Time to go, girls," she said. Our family had made plans to walk together to church on this special holiday.

Aunt Ruthie's white, high-heeled pumps looked smart as they tapped across the driveway. *Tap, tap, tap.* She looked like a model. The skirt of her turquoise dress flowed to her ankles in a hundred pencil-thin pleats. The V neckline framed a pearl necklace. She wore white gloves and held a purse made of milky-looking plastic with a sparkling rhinestone clasp. A turquoise hat balanced on her auburn hair.

Aunt Ruthie, my dad, and their two brothers grew up poor in Chicago, Illinois. They lived in apartments with no hot running water or electricity. They worried a lot about being evicted and coming home from school to find their furniture in the front yard. This morning, though, my aunt looked like a million dollars with no worries.

Uncle Charlie looked handsome in his gray suit, white shirt, and dark tie. A felt hat rested on his head of light brown waves. His shining eyes sported gold-rimmed glasses. He took Aunt Ruthie's hand to help her walk gracefully up the street.

"Hey, Carol Ann," Pete called from his front yard, "Happy Easter and what did the Easter Bunny bring you?"

"Happy Easter to you," I said. "My Easter basket is full of goodies. This morning I ate some jellybeans and part of a marshmallow bunny."

"I ate a handful of jellybeans and a bowlful of oatmeal for breakfast this morning." said Pete. "Wow! Your family group is really agitating the gravel."

"Yeah, we're taking off for church," I said. "Are those new clothes?" Pete's white shirt, tie, and dark slacks looked nice compared to his usual blue jeans.

"Yeah, you like my new threads?" Pete asked. "I hope they look cool for church. Mom told me to keep them clean and neat."

"Your new threads look real cool," I said. "If you see Hey Pup, don't pick him up. He'll leave paw prints up and down your clean white shirt. So, when are you leaving for your church?"

"In a minute," said Pete. "Hawk's driving to church with Ernie and Tim. If I see the puppy, I'll pat his head, but I won't pick him up and mess up my threads."

"Pete…eeeeeeeeeeeeeeeee!" Mary Jane yelled from the porch. "Mom said to get in the car." Pink petticoats puffed out from Mary Jane's pink ruffled chiffon skirt. She adjusted the straw hat on her head of blonde curls. Lucky for her, clean blonde curls swirled around her face. She glared at me, so I raced to catch up with Uncle Charlie.

"Bye, Pete," I called. "Hope to see you later."

"Later gator," he called back.

Lots of families walked to church along La Madera Avenue. Neighborhood trees shimmered in the morning sun. I smelled roses from a neighbor's flower-filled yard. Some noisy kids ran around their yard hunting for hidden Easter eggs.

"I found one," someone shouted.

RUMBLE, RUM, RUM, ROAR.

Ernie's hot rod raced past us like a rocket launched into outer space. The hot rod's big back tires squealed as Ernie roared around the corner onto Cherrylee Drive.

"I hope we never have to stitch up those crazy teenagers when they crash that hot rod," said Aunt Ruthie. "They need to slow down!"

"Aunt Ruthie, that's why Pete's mom doesn't let him ride in Ernie's '32," I said. "She said Ernie will be 'burning rubber' by himself if he doesn't slow down, because Hawk won't be allowed to ride in his 'souped up' car either."

We turned the corner at the flat-roofed Spanish-style house. Families streamed up the street toward our church on the corner of Hemlock Street and Buffington Road.

The Easter fashion parade boasted a pastel rainbow of women dressed in satin, chiffon, and silk. Men wore suits and hats like Uncle Charlie's. White-shirted boys tugged at their ties. Sweet girls, dressed like fragile flowers, clutched dainty purses with white-gloved hands.

"Kathleen," I whispered, "it looks like we're walking in the *Easter Parade* movie with Judy Garland and Fred Astaire. Any minute, someone will start singing, 'Stepping Out, With My Baby.' Then that actress, Ann Miller, will tap dance out of the crowd."

Kathleen nodded her head up and down. She said, "Everyone looks so pretty."

The pastel parade flowed to the steps of our cherished community church. On the front lawn message board, black letters spelled, "For God so loved the world that He gave His only begotten Son, that whosoever believeth in Him should not perish, but have everlasting life. John 3.16."

Trinity Church welcomed us warmly. Through the open sanctuary doors, choir voices sang, "Up from the grave He arose." On the church steps, people hugged and greeted each other.

"I'll take the kids to Bible class, Aunt Ruthie," I volunteered.

"Thank you, Carol Ann," she said, then followed Uncle Charlie.

With cousins on one side of me and sisters on the other, we walked down the ramp toward the breezeway in front of the Bible School classrooms. The kids squirmed excitedly. Bible story cutouts and spring flowers decorated classroom bulletin boards.

Gail gripped my hand and said, "Will you stay with us, Carol Ann? Pwease? You'll like our teacher. Your friends won't miss you this one time. Pwease?"

"Okay," I said and nodded. "Kathleen and I will stay with

you kids today since its Easter. Kathleen, hold Cathie's hand and save us seats while I go talk to my friends."

When I walked out into the breezeway I spotted Roberta, Nancy, Ame, Barbara, and Terry all dressed up in pastel and lace. "Hi girls," I said. "Kathleen and I are staying with the little kids today. Happy Easter and we'll see you next week."

I slipped into Gail's classroom then slipped into a seat next to her, Cathie, and Kathleen. Little Charlie sat behind us with a row of rowdy boys. *It might be fun to be a seven-year-old again for a day,* I thought.

"Welcome children. Happy Easter!" said Gail's teacher, Miss East. "Let's sing a short song, then we'll pray." The teacher began to sing "Jesus Loves Me."

"Jesus loves me, this I know," we all sang out. "For the Bible tells me so." I looked down at sweet Gail. "Little ones to Him belong. They are weak, but He is strong."

When we finished singing, Gail's teacher folded her hands and told us to bow our heads. "Let's pray," she said. "Good morning, God. Thank you for your son, Jesus, and for sending Him to save us from our sins. We celebrate that today, on Easter, and every day. Amen."

After the prayer, Miss East reached for a stack of flannel Bible figures. She spread the colorful flannel pieces on her flannel board. They stuck like magic. Gail's teacher created a scene on her flannel board with felt rocks and a felt tomb. She explained to us that after Jesus died on the cross, they buried him in a tomb like this.

"Is Jesus inside there?" asked one boy on Little Charlie's row of seats.

"Yes, Jerry, but not for long!" Miss East answered.

She opened her King James Bible and read Mark 16:1-8

out loud to the class. Then she continued to move the flannel figures around on the board. She added an angel in a white flowing robe. At first the angel stood in front of the big, brown, felt rock that closed up the tomb, but then the angel rolled the rock aside. The tomb was now open!

Next Miss East added three flannel women to the scene. Two of them were standing and one of them was kneeling down. They had surprised and scared looks on their faces. Gail's teacher explained the women had come to take care of Jesus' body, but instead they saw the open tomb and an angel. The angel told them Jesus was not there because He had risen from the dead!

Jerry interrupted again and said, "So Jesus isn't in the tomb anymore?"

"That's right, Jerry," replied Miss East with a smile. "God raised Jesus from the dead. He is still living today!"

At the end of Bible school, Miss East said, "Remember what Psalm 2:2 says, 'Blessed are all they that put their trust in Him.' Have a happy Resurrection Day. Class dismissed." Kathleen and I grabbed the little kids' hands and went to find Aunt Ruthie and Uncle Charlie.

Parents and children reunited inside the church sanctuary. Families sat together for the Call to Worship at 10:15 A.M. Rows of carved wooden pews flanked a center aisle. Morning light streamed through six windows. By the altar, Reverend Willis Myers placed his Bible and notes on a wooden podium. Over the podium, the altar wall curved up and around displaying some printed words: "Be still and know that I am God. Psalm 46:10." Several rows of benches sat on a raised platform behind the podium.

The choir walked up the steps onto the raised platform.

They filed in quietly toward the benches. Gold scarf-like stoles topped the choir members' long brown robes. We opened our hymnals to page 256 and began to sing.

"On a hill, far away, stood an old rugged cross…," we sang. Our voices, plus the organ music, filled the sanctuary and soared to heaven.

Gail tugged at my arm. She pointed to the cross behind the choir. She whispered in my ear, "Carol Ann, could that be the cross in the song?"

"Sort of," I whispered back, then finished singing "The Old Rugged Cross."

The pastor's message told us all about how Jesus had given His life for our sins. He suffered and died on that "old rugged cross" for all of us. Then, just like Miss East had explained to us in Bible class, Pastor Myers told us Jesus had risen from the dead. That's why we celebrate Easter. Jesus lives so we can too!

Reverend Myers continued by reminding us Jesus meekly walked the roads of earth as God in the flesh and He is the Savior of the world. "Jesus courageously laid down His life for us, because He loves us," Reverend Myers said. "We in turn are to love one another. James 2:8 says, 'If ye fulfill the royal law according to the scripture, thou shalt love thy neighbor as thyself.'"

I smiled really big. *That's what I told Pete yesterday. The Bible says to love our neighbors…even mean ones like Mr. Chester. That's the royal law.* I closed my eyes and prayed. *O God, please bless Mr. Chester and his puppy. Let them have a good Easter.*

"Hallelujah, What a Savior," sang the choir as we left the sanctuary. People streamed through the foyer then outside into the glorious sunshine.

A church elder said to someone, "He is risen."

Someone answered, "He is risen, indeed."

Uncle Charlie shook Reverend Myer's hand. "Fabulous sermon, Pastor," Uncle Charlie complimented.

"Thank you, Dr. Charles," said Reverend Myers. He looked down at us kids. "Be good children today. Help with all the Easter preparations." Then he wagged a finger next to his smiling face, "And don't eat too much candy."

Back at the house, parked cars lined the street: Uncle Charlie's 1948 black Plymouth that looked like a big beetle, Dad's tank, Uncle Johnny's Ford, and Aunt Jean's pale green Pontiac Chieftain cruiser. I liked its Native American Indian-head hood ornament. It shined at night like a brave warrior leading the way down dark, scary streets.

"Oh goodie, the cousins are here. Now we can hunt Easter eggs," said Kathleen as she dashed into the yard. Gail and I followed quickly behind her. The entire family gathered in the front yard for the annual picture.

"Are you ready to get your picture taken?" I asked Gail.

Gail held my hand. "Carol Ann, can I hunt Easter eggs, too, after the pitures?" she asked. Her dimpled, smiling face looked up at me.

"Sure you can, Gail," I said. "After the pictures, I'll help you find lots of eggs."

Kathleen stood in the middle of a giggling group of girls. "Carol Ann…Gail, stand by Pamela and Sandy," said Aunt Ruthie as she arranged her daughter, Cathie, between Kathleen and me. Uncle Charlie patiently held his camera.

"Cathie, your dress and matching hat look so pretty," said cousin Pamela.

After the pictures, I helped Gail and cousin Cathie hunt Easter eggs in our play yard. Dad stood on the sidewalk filming us with his movie camera. I wondered if a movie camera would ever capture my dad's tall, dark, and handsome good looks. *Could Dad be a movie star someday?* Gail got her good looks and dimples from Dad. *I look more like Dad's brother, Uncle Johnny.*

"Lucky me, I found one," a cousin yelled. "I found a cute puppy, too!"

Hey Pup joined the hunt. The pup and kids looked for the hidden, colorfully dyed, hard-boiled eggs. Cousins darted around, digging through bushes, and looking in planters. A yellow egg, perched on top of the chicken car, looked like a baby chick.

I helped Hey Pup and the kids hunt for eggs while picking up a few for myself. Hey Pup sniffed at some eggs sitting on the slide steps. I picked him up with one arm and used the other to climb up the slide. Up on top, I waved at Pete and the teens in their yard then *whoooooooosh* down we flew. My bangs and the puppy's ears waved in the air.

Dad said, "Gail, walk this way. Look at the camera and show me your dimples."

Hey Pup and I walked over to Dad. Gail smiled proudly as she stepped toward us. Her plastic bucket was overflowing with colored eggs…until she tripped and fell down.

Crunch. Crunch. Crackle. Crunch. Crunch. Woof. Sniff. Sniff.

Yikes. Poor, Gail. I tried not to laugh at her when she stood up covered in colored eggshells. Smashed yolks and whites were crumbled on her yellow dress. Dad's shaking shoulders betrayed his laughter as he hid his face behind the camera. I tried really hard to still my shaking shoulders. Hey Pup wandered over to Gail and sniffed. *Sniff, sniff, sniff.*

"My eggs," Gail wailed. She looked into her empty bucket then at the mess on the ground. "My eggs are all mashed and the puppy's eating them!"

"Take my eggs," I offered, as I brushed the front of her dress. Then I ran with Hey Pup to the backyard, pushed the pup under the fence, and fled to Aunt Ruthie's kitchen. Helping in a busy kitchen beat dealing with a messy, egg-covered kid.

Our early afternoon dinner was set out buffet-style in Aunt Ruthie's kitchen. The food spread across the kitchen table and onto the countertops. The feast featured a ham, vegetables, casseroles, potato salad, coleslaw, gelatin salad, and relishes that smelled like onions. Cartoon chicks and bunnies paraded around a cottage-cheese container filled with white curds. A fragrant floral centerpiece decorated the table.

Mom, the aunts, and Granny Mary bustled like busy bunnies around the kitchen. They wore fancy aprons over their fancy dresses. Aunt Jean laid out several fruit salads, including Mom's Ambrosia salad made with marshmallows, pineapple, and coconut. *Yum.*

"Food's ready," Aunt Jean called to the men.

"Fabulous," said Uncle Charlie.

"Wow, pineapple upside-down cake," I said. "I have dibs on a BIG piece." I stared hungrily at Aunt Jean's chocolate cake, assorted pastries on a china platter, a banana pudding, and a tray of my mom's cookies: chocolate chip, oatmeal, molasses, and crescents dipped in powdered sugar. *Yum. Where do I start?* I thought.

I eyeballed our entire Easter feast. Pete would say, 'Let's

dig in.' And everybody did after Uncle Charlie led us in a prayer of thanks for God's many blessings.

Gail walked through the kitchen clutching her Easter basket. A smear of chocolate and some crumbled, yucky yolks smudged the front of her dress. "Mom is outside on the patio, Gail," I told her. Poor Gail disappeared in that direction.

"What's buzzin', cuzzin?" Pete asked from the doorway. "What a bash!"

"It is a great party. Get a plate and dig in with the buzzin' cuzzins," I offered.

We lined up behind Uncle Johnny and Aunt Marilyn. At six-foot-five, Dad's fraternal twin brother, Johnny, looked different than Dad though he also had tall, dark, and handsome good looks. His wife, Aunt Marilyn, stood next to him holding Baby Barbara on her skirted hip.

Covered in red lipstick, Aunt Marilyn's lips looked like the red, puffy, wax lips we bought at the candy store. I liked to put those fake lips on my lips so I could look like Aunt Marilyn. But, Pete said they looked dumb.

"Gail Ruth Hartnell, where are you?" Mom called frantically as she entered the room. "Have you seen her, Carol Ann? I've looked everywhere for her."

"She walked through the kitchen a little while ago," I said. "I sent her out to the patio to find you, Mom. I didn't see her after that." *Where's my little sister? She fell down and crushed her eggs, wandered through the kitchen in a dirty daze, and now she's missing. I should've helped her. Could Hey Pup find Gail with his big black nose?*

Pete put his plate down. "Let's go find her, Carol Ann."

"Mr. Chester wouldn't pay us back by hurting a little kid, would he?" I asked Pete and shivered. *O God, please help us find Gail,* I prayed.

"Mr. Chester's scary and crazy but not that crazy," said Pete. "Did anyone check in your house?"

"I'm sure they did, but let's check again," I said. *Be brave little sister,* I prayed.

"Gailllllllllllllllllllllllllllllllll," we called as we looked in my parents' bedroom.

A soft moan escaped into the hallway. Pete and I looked at each other. A pink plastic bunny and some jellybeans littered the floor in Gail's bedroom.

Pete said, "You've either got a bear living in that bedroom or a sleeping kid under that pile of covers." He bravely pulled the blankets back.

There was Gail sleeping soundly in her crusty, crumpled chiffon dress. An Easter basket was snuggled next to her. Chocolate and other gooey stuff smeared her face and hands.

"Thank the LORD, you found her," Mom cried. "I was sick from worrying."

"You can stop worrying, Mrs. H.," said Pete. "Mystery solved."

"Thanks for helping, Pete," I said. "You deserve a reward. Want a cookie? Mom made the crescent cookies you love...the ones dipped in powdered sugar."

"Sure," Pete said. We ran flat out back to Aunt Ruthie's kitchen and the Easter dessert table. "When can I give my mom the crescent cookie recipe?"

"I'll write down the recipe for you," I said. "I know it by heart."

Pete nodded his head as he munched a cookie and mumbled, "I already know part of the recipe: when the cookies cool off, you dip them in powdered sugar, and then gobble them up like this." Pete popped a powdered piece of cookie between his open lips.

I bet Hey Pup would enjoy a dog treat as much as Pete is enjoying Mom's cookies. Is the puppy okay? Does Mr. Chester give him treats?

Chapter Eight

Vaccine Views

Wednesday, April 13th, meant only half of our Easter break remained. I stretched my arms up over my head and got out of bed. Sunlight streamed into our bedroom around the window shade. I pulled it down and let go. *Shhsllaap.* The shade disappeared under a pink valance on top of the window. Then I pulled the other shade. *Shhsllaap.*

"I'm asleep, Carol Ann," Kathleen grumbled. She ducked under the covers.

"Time to rise and shine," I said as I tugged at her blanket. She kicked my hand with her foot. "Get up, so I can stop bugging you."

From the other room, Mom said, "Get up girls, get dressed, and stop fighting."

Kathleen crawled out of bed, gave me a dirty look, and tattled to Mom, "Carol Ann's teasing me." Sometimes it felt good to tease someone until they ratted on you.

"Sorry," I said as I started making our twin beds. Pink ruffled bedspreads matched the window curtains and valance. Our bedroom and our den, with the old black and white television set, shared one long room. Dad's color TV sat out in the living room. When family visited, they slept on the scratchy gray sofa that divided the room in half. Pete said I had a cool pad for a bedroom. A wall divided my "cool pad" from a one-car garage.

Since the television shared our space, I planned to watch it today. After our chores, we could watch an old movie or some cartoons like *Bugs Bunny, Daffy Duck, Porky Pig, Little Lulu,* and *Mighty Mouse.* My cool mom let us watch a lot of television during our Easter break. *I Love Lucy* would be fun to watch, too.

"Kathleen, you want to watch Esther Williams with me in a little while?" I asked my sister. "One of her movies is on this morning. Mom saw it listed in the *TV Guide.*"

"I'll watch it, if you stop teasing me, Carol Ann," she said. I stopped teasing and we watched the movie together.

After lunch, the warm sunshine outside felt like an early summer. I finished eating a molasses cookie. *Yum.* I happily sat on top of the slide. Down below, my sisters dragged our blow-up swimming pool across the grass.

"Carol Ann, help us," the kids called to me from their pool pile. That poor collapsed pool needed a lot of breath to blow it up. The girls ran around in their ruffled bathing suits trying to straighten out the pool. Hey Pup ran between their skinny ankles.

"I'll be down in a minute," I said. "Don't step on the puppy."

Today felt like 90 degrees outside. My legs stuck to the

hot slide. I wiped sweat from my face. I needed a swimming pool right now. On television, Esther Williams always looked beautiful in her sparkling bathing suit as she glided through her swimming routine. Water ballet would be fun. I lifted my arms and stroked them through the air like a swimmer would. My moving arms fanned my hot face as I gracefully stroked the sky.

The grooving sounds of "Bo Diddley" blasted out of Hawk's transistor radio next door. "Bo Diddley, Bo Diddley, have you heard…" I looked down at Pete's yard. Hopefully, no one saw me pretend swimming to the rock and roll tune.

The front of Hawk's Ford Slant back stuck out of the garage. The chrome grill gleamed on the front of the red-orange car. I stared at the car. Mary Jane stared at the teens. Pete called her "boy crazy." His mom worried about her boy crazy daughter. I worried that Mary Jane saw me swimming up on the slide.

Click, click, tap, tap, click, tapped Mary Jane's tap shoes on the concrete.

She must have dance practice today. I'm glad my dance class got cancelled. Pete ran out the back door tossing a baseball. *I guess baseball practice didn't get cancelled.* He stopped for a minute to admire the paint job on Hawk's Ride. The red-orange paint sparkled in the sun. Mary Jane looked up at me. She started laughing.

"Hey, Carol Ann, you wanna toss this baseball around?" Pete yelled up at me.

"Sure," I said. I let go of the railing and slid down the slide.

Pete walked through the gate and stopped at the swimming pool. Kathleen blew into it. The rolled sides puffed up a little bit with each breath. Pete's sister, Mandy, Gail, Little Charlie, and Cathie wiggled and watched Kathleen. The puppy wagged his tail.

"We need more breaff, Carol Ann," said Gail. "Kathleen's running out."

"I'll help you," I said. "Pete, wait a minute while I give them some of my *breaff.*"

"No sweat," he said. "I'll help, too."

I wiped slobber off the nozzle then I blew into the pool. The kids jumped up and down excitedly. I stopped blowing. My face felt hot and puffy like the pool.

"Cool it, Carol Ann," said Pete. "Go rest a minute. Your face looks like a red tomato. This gig is made in the shade." He took over and finished the job. *Oops, now Pete's sweaty face looks like a smiling, red tomato.* "Get the hose, kids, and fill 'er up."

"Thanks, Pete," I said. "The kids will have a wet and wild blast in their pool."

Their small feet danced around the swirling water that filled the pool. *That should keep them busy part of the day. I might take a dip later, too, in case I need to clean off puppy slobber.*

"Like wow! That looks like fun," said Pete. He straightened his baseball cap and said, "Think fast, Carol Ann." His baseball flew towards me and then past me. The other thing flying across the grass at me had four legs and two floppy ears.

"Hey Pup," I said, "Go chase Pete's baseball." He did. He ran after the ball like a tri-colored tornado. The swimmers turned to watch the pup. He stopped at the still ball and barked. *Woof. Woof. Ahwooooo.* Then he bounced and barked at it some more.

Pete scooped him up with one hand and grabbed the baseball with the other. "Hey Pup is just like Gramp's dog. He loves to chase things." Pete held the pup up to his face and told him, "This is my baseball. It doesn't have rabbit ears. You were bred to hunt rabbits. You can run for miles and you have a boss sniffer…your nose."

"I just hope Mr. Chester appreciates his pup like we do, "I said. "You forgot to mention another thing that Beagle pups do. They escape their yard all the time."

The kids called from the blow-up pool, "Show us the puppy, pleeeeease."

Pete bent over the pool to show off Hey Pup. "Sincerely" by the McGuire Sisters floated over the fence. I would sincerely love to own Hey Pup but that was impossible.

"The McGuire Sisters have good sounds," said Pete as he put the puppy on the ground. A splash of water startled the pup. "I really dig them. I think they're great."

"Me, too," I shouted above the splashing, screaming kids behind me.

"Mary Jane wondered if you always practice swimming up on the slide," Pete said. "I told her you practice flying like John Wayne in *The Flying Tigers* movie."

My face blushed. "Kathleen and I watched an old Esther William's movie this morning. I was moving my arms like Esther Williams did in the movie," I said.

"Mom watched that flick this morning while she did her housework," Pete said. "I wondered why she back-stroked across our living room."

"Yikes," I said, "your poor Mom. I hope you didn't laugh at her."

"No," said Pete. "I made myself scarce, like the Invisible Man."

"Pete…eeeeeeeeeeeee!" Mary Jane yelled then appeared at the gate. "Mom wants you. We're late for practice. Hawk's driving his car, and Tim is riding along with us."

BRUMMM, BRUM, BRUM, rumbled Hawk's car next to the vine-covered fence.

"Bye, Pete. Have fun riding to practice in Hawk's Ride," I said. I walked over to the pool and sat down between squirming kids. The water felt cool on my warm skin. I dribbled water on the puppy. He licked his dripping face and wagged his tail for more.

"Carol Ann, can we play paper dolls after we dry off?" Gail asked.

"Okay," I said. "When we're all dried off and after I've taken Hey Pup back home, then we'll play paper dolls. He would eat my paper dolls and that could hurt him."

Later in the afternoon, after we had dried off, we opened my box of paper dolls. We spread them around on the area rug in Aunt Ruthie's living room. My precious Betsy McCall paper dolls looked happy in their perfect, paper world.

Ever since 1952, when the paper dolls first appeared in *McCall's Magazine*, I'd been collecting them. I liked their flat, safe world. Betsy didn't worry about shots, or polio, or car accidents. She didn't need courage. In her world, she never ducked under a school desk or covered her neck during a duck and cover drill like we did.

"Beware of the tabs on their clothes," I warned. "They rip easily. Betsy's dad wears a permanent suit so we don't dress him." We laid out the different Betsy McCall stories and pretended to be Betsy, her cousins, and friends. *Am I too old for paper dolls?* I wondered. As long as Mary Jane didn't see me, I could visit with Betsy McCall in safety. If she saw me with paper dolls, she'd call me a baby. Then she'd tell the whole school.

Aunt Ruthie walked through the living room toward the patio. "You children are playing so nicely. You're being such a good boy, Little Charlie. That's an interesting face you put on Mr. Potato Head. Oh Cathie, Betsy looks beautiful."

The girls didn't even look up. Their busy fingers busily moved Betsy and friends around in the paper world sprawled all over the floor. Betsy even had a dog. *I wish I did*.

From out on the patio, voices drifted into the living room through the open window next to the fireplace. My nosey ears listened.

"Would you like some water or juice?" Aunt Ruthie asked one of her friends.

Uncle Charlie asked someone, "Did your friend get that job in town?"

"He starts at Lockheed Aircraft Company next week. He's excited about his new job," a male voice answered.

"That's wonderful," said Aunt Ruthie. "You must invite him over for barbecued ribs sometime soon. You know how much Charlie likes to make his special ribs."

The smell from those special ribs floated through the window. My mouth watered. Barbecued ribs sure were tasty. Lucky for us, our dinner cooked just outside on Uncle Charlie's grill. We'd eat ribs with white bread. *Yum.* Hopefully, Hey Pup wouldn't pick up their scent and run over to investigate. He sure liked to follow his nose. People food isn't good for dogs. Kibble keeps dogs healthy. *Will the pup sit for a doggie treat?*

Uncle Charlie laughed. He said, "My barbecued ribs are a poor substitute for the ribs we used to get at Tippton's Ribs in Tulsa, Oklahoma. When we were kids, my brother, Lewis, and I devoured ribs by the dozens. Tipptons served the best barbecued ribs, with white bread, plus lots of extra sauce on the side."

I played paper dolls as I listened to the adults continue to talk. They sounded interesting and smart. They worked at L.A. County Hospital, too. If their talk got too scary, though, I'd stop listening. They talked about concrete blast-resistant houses, smog, cancer, the latest cars, and the price of gasoline. One lady loved her new vacuum. *The Seven Little Foys* movie, starring Bob Hope, would be in theaters soon.

"Would anyone like more juice?" Aunt Ruthie asked.

"I'd like more pineapple juice, if you don't mind," a woman's voice said.

For a moment, I stopped listening to the grown-ups and thought about my aunt as a teenager. Dad had shared with me that his sister Ruth worked in a defense plant during World War II yet still attended high school. Her salary paid the electric bill. Dad and his twin brother, John, could listen to *The Shadow* and *The Bing Crosby Show* on their radio. Aunt Ruthie was a good big sister!

On many nights Ruth had to ask her mother to make the boys turn the radio down, so she could study. At age 16, Ruth graduated from Kelly High School with the highest scholastic rating ever achieved in Chicago schools. She received a full scholarship to college and used her incredible intelligence to become a doctor of pathology.

I heard a man's voice ask, "I know you can't talk about your research, Ruth, but what do you think about the announcement yesterday? Did you watch it on your TV?"

"Yes, I watched it. I think it's wonderful. What a breakthrough. We've been waiting for Dr. Salk's announcement. The lab buzzed about the news all day long."

Uncle Charlie spoke up. "KTTV, Channel 11, moved tons of equipment to Ann Arbor, Michigan. They did a terrific job broadcasting the live coverage of the official National Foundation for Infantile Paralysis Conference. Dr. Jonas Salk, his team, and the University of Pittsburgh deserve our thanks for discovering a life-saving polio vaccine."

"He's a national hero," someone said. "The University must be so proud."

An excited voice said, "All that fundraising by the National Foundation for Infantile Paralysis really paid off. Now, all those March of Dimes poster children and children everywhere have something to smile about." *I'm not smiling about getting a polio vaccine.*

Uncle Charlie said, "It's fabulous. Hundreds of scientists and polio experts gathered at the University of Michigan. I wish Ruth and I could have flown there to witness history. On TV, we watched Dr. Francis of Ann Arbor, Michigan, share the news of Dr. Salk's polio vaccine. Dr. Salk's results are remarkable."

"What an achievement!" someone said. "His discovery is monumental."

I leaned back against the fireplace hearth. My heart pounded. The girls still played quietly. They weren't eavesdropping like me. *Wow, Dr. Salk's vaccine proved it could stop polio! Kids won't get sick with polio anymore! Uh oh, that vaccine could be the shot that Pete teased me about. Yikes. Be brave, Carol Ann, during this scary spring.*

Aunt Ruthie said, "Now that it's official, I'd like to order some vaccine from Cutter Labs up in Berkeley and get our kids vaccinated."

"I don't know, Ruth," said Uncle Charlie. "I'd like to see those effectiveness percentages go up first. We'll talk about it later. Let me check the ribs so we can eat."

"Whhhhhuuuuu," I breathed out. *Good old Uncle Charlie saved the day like Mighty Mouse. I'd rather hear the grown-ups talk about their vaccine views than view the vaccine in a shot ready to hurt my arm. The shot pot will stay in the kitchen cupboard. No stings today. Hooray! But someday soon there might be! How soon? I wondered.*

Chapter Nine

Dan's Diner

BRUMMM, BRUMMM roared Hawk's Ride next door. One of the teens cranked up the radio. The R&B song, "Hound Dog" by Willie Mabon blasted across the fence. Car doors slammed. The teens must be going somewhere. *BRUMMM*.

The startled puppy jumped in my arms as I sat down on one of our swings. I patted his head as I pushed the swing back and forth with my feet. "It's okay puppy," I said. "The teens won't hurt you. They're listening to your song about a hound dog."

"Hi Carol Ann. Hi pup," said Pete as he walked through the side gate and sat in a swing next to mine. He pushed his feet on the ground with running steps to move the swing. Up and back and up flew the swing toward the sky. His hands gripped the chains.

"The pup and I are hanging out and listening to some great tunes," I said.

"Listen to that boss tune about a hound dog," said Pete as he swooshed by. "Do you think the pup knows that tune's about him? Nah, he doesn't."

I twirled the canvas seat of the swing around. The chain above me twisted tighter and tighter. I held onto Hey Pup with one hand and the chain with the other. When I picked up my feet the pup and I twirled like a twister. I put my feet down to stop us.

"I think this pup is pretty smart, but he can't understand most of our people words. He's smart enough to sit when I offer him a treat," I said.

"Hey Pup might sit, but he doesn't stop howling when we tell him 'No,'" said Pete as he slowed down his swing to a stop. "He's a hound dog alright."

An afternoon breeze brushed by us and ruffled Mom's laundry hanging on the nearby clothesline. The pup strained his head to see the waving laundry. He'd make of mess of Mom's clean clothes if he pulled them down. Now he strained his head the other direction to watch the kids. *Woof, woof, woof* he barked softly.

My sisters and cousins raced on the sidewalk, across the lawn, and over to the monkey bars. *Screech, screech*, squawked some chickens by the chicken car. Hey Pup squirmed to get out of my arms. He wanted to chase chickens.

"Where are the teens going?" I asked as I stood up.

Pete jumped up out of the swing and walked over to the monkey bars. He climbed up on top of a bar and hung up-side-down. "Hawk and the guys are heading over to Dan's Diner. My mom is gonna drop Mary Jane and me over there on her way to town. The Diner is our dinner destination. Mom's picking us up on her way home."

"You're a lucky duck to get dropped off there," I said. "We're having soup and homemade rolls for supper. Mom made some oatmeal cookies, too."

Pete said, "I hope you're gonna save me some of your mom's cookies."

"I will 'cause you're the Munch Mouth of La Madera Avenue," I said.

"Very funny, Carol Ann," said Pete. "I'll be thinking of you when I dip my fries in ketchup and slurp a triple chocolate shake at Dan's Diner."

"That's so mean. You know how much I love those shakes." I set the puppy down and pulled doggie treats from my pocket. The treats looked like miniature, brown, dog bones. "Look what the pup can do for a treat. We've been working on this."

I kneeled down on the grass, looked in the puppy's beady, black eyes, and said, "Sit." Hey Pup wagged his tail, turned in a circle, and laid down. Then he rolled over and kicked his four white legs in the air like an overturned bug.

"Wow!" said Pete. "The pup did everything except what you asked him to do." Pete kneeled down, patted the pup and said, "You're a clever, little fellow."

"Pete...eeeeeee!" yelled Mary Jane as she walked through the gate into my yard. "There you are. Mom says we've got to go now. Why's the puppy playing dead?"

"He's doing some tricks for treats," I said. "He's trying to sit."

"Looks like you need more training than the puppy," said Mary Jane.

Squawk, squawk, screeched a chicken as it ran down the sidewalk toward my backyard and Mr. Chester's fence. Hey

Pup popped up very much alive and raced after that chicken like a racecar heading for the finish line. *Woof, woof* he barked as he ran. He disappeared around the corner of the house and then we heard *awhoooooooooooooooo!*

"What's that awful noise?" asked Pete's older sister.

"It's the baby hound dog," said Pete. "That's what hounds like to do…howl. First they chase their prey and then they howl when they catch or corner it."

A commotion started on the monkey bars as the little kids jumped down and raced past the chicken car towards the front yard. Gail yelled, "Uncle Charlie's home. We heard his car. We wanna go to the…dine-ner place for a treat!"

Mary Jane moved toward the gate waving her arm at Pete. "Mom's waiting for us," she said. "Let's leave so Carol Ann can run with the kiddies or the puppy."

"Okay, I'm behind you," said Pete as he waved to me. "See ya later, alligator."

"After while, crocodile," I said back to Pete as I waved goodbye.

A new commotion moved in my direction. The kids surrounded Uncle Charlie as he walked my way. They jumped around him like a pack of puppies. He smiled down at them as he patted Little Charlie's head and held Cathie's hand.

"Hi Carol Ann," said Uncle Charlie. "The kids want me to take them over to Dan's Diner for supper. What do you think of that plan?"

"I like that plan," I said, "but Mom made vegetable soup and rolls for supper."

"Guess what," said my uncle, "why don't we go to the diner and let the moms eat the soup. I'm hungry for one of Dan's greasy, grilled cheese sandwiches and a shake."

"Yeah, me, too," said Little Charlie. "I want some fries with ketchup."

"Me too, me too," chorused the kids all at once.

"Everybody grab your jackets while I talk to Ruth and Jeanne," said Uncle Charlie with a big grin on his face. "Meet at my car in fifteen minutes."

Uncle Charlie's big, black car waited on the driveway as I herded the kids toward it. I thought that the 1948 Plymouth looked like a giant, black beetle. We climbed inside and sat down on the scratchy gray seats. We waited patiently while Uncle Charlie talked to the moms. Good old Uncle Charlie loved to have fun. Maybe he'd take us on a drive through the gravel pits after supper. His car rolled on the pit road like a rollercoaster.

The kids jumped up and down excitedly as Uncle Charlie strolled toward us. He smiled, waved, and whistled while he walked. That jingling noise sounded like his keys. When he climbed in the driver's seat, we cheered. When my uncle cut out of the driveway, "Oh Happy Day," by The Four Knights, filled the car with music.

Uncle Charlie found a parking space in the crowded diner parking lot. The lighted DINER sign stood 20 feet above the ground. An arrow pointed at the entrance door surrounded by a black and white checkerboard design. We followed my uncle into the diner and looked for a crowd-sized booth. I smelled great, greasy, good diner aromas.

Inside Dan's Diner, red vinyl booths, paired with chrome-edged tables, lined the walls. Framed Americana posters hung on the wall space over each booth. In one corner, an American flag fluttered from an eagle-topped flagpole. Round tables, with red and chrome chairs, were scattered around the room on the wall-to-wall black and white checkered floor. A waitress carried a tray loaded with shakes and burgers.

"Like wow," I whispered to my sisters. "I love this place! It's the coolest place in town!"

Lots of teenagers danced in the diner's back corner. The rock and roll tune, "We're Gonna Rock Around the Clock," blasted out of the record-filled jukebox. Music flowed in waves around the room as the teens swirled and dipped.

Uncle Charlie motioned us to a spot near the front windows. We could see all the action in the parking lot. Our group piled into the booth and scooted around the table. Gail and Kathleen bounced on the seat as a smiling waitress handed out menus. Her red striped uniform with the white apron looked crisp and professional.

From inside a rectangular opening on the back wall, Dan, the owner, nodded and waved to us with his spatula. A different uniformed waitress worked in the space between the utility counter and the eating counter. She smiled at us as she clipped several orders to a metal spinner near the cook's head.

A Mother's March for Polio poster hung over the coffee percolator. Tim helped Hawk put up that poster and others like it all over town. Polio seemed far from this place, unless you glanced in Tim's direction. He sat with Hawk and Ernie at a table. Tim's crutches leaned by his chair. He tapped his fingers on the table to the jukebox's rock and roll tune.

Whirrrrrrrrrrr. The great, green milkshake machine spun ice cream, milk, and flavorings into silky, smooth shakes. The waitress reached into a glass pie keeper and retrieved a slice of chocolate pie with mile-high meringue. *Yum.* Assorted cake and pie slices sat on plates on glass shelves in the round dessert holder.

"I don't know what you kiddos are having for supper, but I'm getting a grilled cheese, fries, and a triple-thick chocolate shake," announced Uncle Charlie.

"I want the same!" said every voice at the table. "Let's order." And we did. The waitress smiled as she jotted down our orders on her tablet.

Gail tugged at my pleated skirt and said, "I can't weed the menu, Carol Ann."

I smiled at her and said, "That's okay, Gail. Lots of kids your age can't read yet."

"And I'm one of them," said Pete, laughing, as he sat down next to me. "I know the menu by heart, so I don't have to read it. Hi, everyone. We're sitting over by the dance floor. I saw you cruise in. Glad you could 'make the scene' at Dan's Diner."

"We're glad, too," I said. "There's a crowd here tonight. This is unreal."

At the counter, some rough-looking boys sat on mushroom-shaped barstools that looked like they sprouted from the floor. The boys swiveled around and around like tops. Their jellyroll hairdos looked as greasy as…greasy jellyrolls. A blond-haired boy combed his hair as he stared at me with narrowed eyes. I looked away first. He looked like *bad* news.

"Who are those boys over there?" I whispered to Pete. "They're scary looking."

"Those guys *are* scary," said Pete in a soft voice. "They have a car club called The Cruisers. Hawk knows them from school." Pete turned to my uncle and asked, "May Carol Ann walk back to our table with me? She can watch the dancers up close while she waits for her food. I'll watch for your signal that the grub has landed."

Uncle Charlie said, "Go on, Carol Ann, and I'll signal when the food has arrived."

I walked a little closer to Pete as we passed by The Cruisers. The blond jelly roller reached out and stopped Pete. *Yikes.* I gulped in alarm. *What will that kid do to my friend? What will that kid do to me? O God, help us please.* Now all three raunchy-looking boys stood up in a menacing manner. *Gulp.*

They reminded me of someone...Oh, yeah. They reminded me of Mr. Chester. I smelled a strong, sweaty smell. They wore T-shirts tucked into stained denim jeans tucked into black boots. The teens acted aggressively with loud remarks and tough attitudes.

Pete said, "What's up guys? Hey Butch, your Merc is real cool. I eyeballed it out in the parking lot. It's a chrome-plated machine. Could I have a ride sometime?"

"What are you two ankle-biters doing in our territory?" asked the blond jelly roller as he looked at Pete then at me. "Hey, Shrimp, is she your girlfriend? Ha, ha, ha."

Pete said, "I thought this diner was Dan's territory. And, hey, she's my friend."

Hawk walked into the ever-growing group surrounding us. Even Tim limped over on his crutches. Dan glanced from the kitchen. I saw him frown. The Cruisers better not mess with Dan. He had years of Marine training and could take care of these troublemakers like Mighty Mouse took care of the bad cats.

"Hi Butch," said Hawk. "You got a question for my brother? If not, tell your friend to let go of Pete and Carol Ann."

"Hi Hawk," said Butch. "We were just talking to the kid. We don't want trouble."

"Speak for yourself, Butch," said the terrible teen with the blond jellyroll.

The tune, "What'cha Gonna Do," by The Drifters, rolled out of the jukebox. It made me think, *what is this angry teenager gonna do? What will Dan do if a fight starts?*

Uncle Charlie rose up off the booth seat. *What will Uncle Charlie do to protect us?* Big Dan pushed through his kitchen door just as two uniformed police officers pushed through the diner's door. The officers walked in, looked around, and strolled over to the crowd around Pete and me.

One officer tipped his hat in Dan's direction and asked, "What's going on? Do we need to bust up a fight?" The policemen towered over The Cruisers. The rough boys looked like sticks next to two oak trees. The blond stick squirmed and stepped back.

Dan shook hands with the police officers and said, "There's no trouble here. These boys were just leaving." Butch threw some money on the counter, motioned to his buddies, and walked to the entry door.

The blond jelly roller mumbled, "It's time to split when the HEAT gets here."

The Cruisers walked out the door and into the night. *ROAR, ROAR, ROAR* roared from outside as a car started up. Tires squealed when the car peeled out of the parking lot. The kids turned from looking out of the window and waved at me from our table. Then their straws slurped up shakes and their fingers dipped fries in ketchup. Was my shake safe from sneaky fingers and straws?

"Your food is here, Carol Ann," called my uncle. "Are you okay?"

"Yes, thanks, Uncle Charlie," I said. "I'll be there in a

minute."

The different diners scattered as I moved in to where Pete now sat at the counter. "Are *you* okay?" I asked Pete. "Were you scared?"

"Aw, I wasn't scared," said Pete. "They just wanted to talk. The blond guy got a little rough. He's a real oddball…he's not normal. A fight was brewing like Dan's coffee on the counter. The policemen saved the day before Hawk had to step in and help us out."

"I watched Tim limp over to lend a hand…or a crutch. He could have bopped them on their heads and knocked them out with one blow," I said and laughed.

"I'm glad Tim didn't have to resort to violence," Pete said. "The Cruisers' gig…you know their fun…got "shot down" so they split."

Handsome Hawk patted Pete's back and said, "You handled yourself real good, kid. I'm proud of you. You wanna celebrate with a banana split? It's on me."

"Gee thanks, Hawk," answered Pete.

"Sure, kid. See you back at our table. Bye, Carol Ann," said Hawk as he left us.

"Like wow, Pete, you had a ton of courage in front of those guys," I said.

"That wasn't courage. I was bluffing," said Pete. "It felt like three hounds had a chicken cornered, and I was the chicken. *Cluck, cluck, cluck.*"

"You didn't look scared or chicken. I was glad to hide behind you. Those teens reminded me of Mr. Chester," I said. "When the blond one talked about their "territory," I thought of Mr. Chester prowling his fence. They acted like angry, growling, junkyard dogs prowling Dan's Diner. Even their greasy hair stuck up funny like Mr. Chester's."

"Yeah, really," said Pete. "I'd better go and eat my banana split now. See ya later."

I waved goodbye to Pete. "Papa Loves Mambo," by Perry Como, propelled a crowd of dancers out onto the floor. I watched Pete walk back to his table dodging elbows, full skirts, and dancing feet as teens twirled.

I returned to the table to eat. My fries were cold and my chocolate shake had swallowed the whipped cream that topped it, but I still enjoyed each bite and slurp.

I followed my family out of Dan's Diner. We had a blast…a good time, before and after the bad time. Back in Uncle Charlie's car, I watched the DINER sign fade into the distance behind us. Hawk's Ride and Ernie's '32 were still parked in front.

"That was a fabulous meal," said Uncle Charlie from behind the steering wheel. "Dan grills a great sandwich. Are you kiddos ready to shake up those shakes in your stomachs with a wild ride through the gravel pits?"

"Yes, we are!" shouted the kids. "Go, go, go!" *Shaking like a leaf tonight when I stood next to Pete and those bad boys is all the shaking I want to do,* I thought.

The Cruisers scared us tonight. *Will they ever scare us again? I sure hope not.* I leaned back onto the scratchy seat of Uncle Charlie's car. The Cruisers go to high school here in town and they probably know where Pete lives! *Yikes. Will this scary spring ever end? Or, maybe I should say, how will this scary spring end?*

Chapter Ten

Front Yard Fun

Ting a ling a ling a ling. Ting a ling a ling a ling.

"The ice cream man is here!" someone yelled.

I jingled the quarters in my pocket. Neighbor kids swarmed onto the street like ants at a picnic. My cousins, sisters, and I swarmed out there, too.

"Everybody better know what they want," I warned them.

Ting a ling, a ling, a ling.

Gail and Mandy jumped around. "I want a sunny cone," said Gail.

"Me too," echoed Mandy.

"Girls, call it a Sundae Cone," I said. "It is a waffle cone filled with vanilla ice cream and topped with chocolate and peanuts."

"That's it," said Gail. "That's what I want."

The boxy, white truck slowed to a stop in front of our house. A sign on the truck's side pictured all of its treats: *Ice*

Cream Bars, Toasted Almond bars, Strawberry Shortcake bars, Chocolate Éclair bar, and the *Sundae Cone*. They all looked so yummy!

"Hello," said the ice cream man as he climbed from his truck. "What can I get for you out of my freezer?"

In front of us, a line of children wiggled like a worm then crowded around the back of the truck. The ice cream man, in his crisp, white uniform and cap, waited patiently for every order. When he opened the freezer door, icy air blasted us. Children paid for delicious delights. They walked away smiling, licking, and biting treats. The ice cream man clicked the coin changer hanging from his belt.

Cha Ching, Cha Ching, Cha Ching.

Pete popped into the line behind us. "This must be fat city," he said. "Everyone's smiling. They're in good humor. You know, *Good…Humor…Ice Cream.*"

"You're funny, Pete," I said. "Is it true? Is that what *Good Humor* stands for?"

"The guy who invented *Good Humor Ice Cream* wanted people to enjoy his ice cream treats and be in a good humor, you know, happy. That's what my grandpa told me. Slurping on a *Toasted Almond* bar makes me happy and in…good humor."

"I'm happy," said Kathleen as she moved forward in line.

Finally our turn arrived. The ice cream man opened his freezer. He pulled out our treats: *Ice Cream Bars* for Kathleen and Little Charlie, *Sundae Cones* for Gail, Mandy, and Cathie, an *Almond Toasted bar* for Pete, and a pink *Strawberry Shortcake* bar for me!

"I'm happy," I said. Very carefully, I bit into the crunchy cake coating of my ice cream bar. I savored its sweet, strawberry pink filling.

"I'm digging this *Toasted Almond* bar," said Pete as he bit off a frozen chunk, "But maybe next time I'll try the *Chocolate Éclair.*"

RUMBLE, RUM, RUM.

Ernie cruised up behind the ice cream truck. "Mr. Sandman," by The Chordettes, vibrated out of Ernie's '32. Hawk waved his arm to motion Pete over to the car.

Hawk said, "Here's some bread. Get us two *Ice Cream Bars* and keep the change."

"Thanks, Hawk," said Pete as he walked back to the ice cream truck.

"Let's go sit down, Carol Ann," chorused the kids. Their sticky fingers pointed to our blanket on the grass. "Last one there is a rotten egg," someone shouted. I sat down on the blanket to enjoy my ice cream. The kids sat all around me. They sucked, and slurped, and swallowed their treats while skinny ice cream streams flowed down their arms.

While I bit into the sweetest strawberry treat, the sweetest puppy bounded up to me. He licked drips on the blanket. "What are you doing out of your yard again?" I asked. "Did you hear the Ice Cream Man?"

"Oh, Ice Cream Man, don't leave yet," Mary Jane called from her driveway. "Debbie and I want two *Sundae Cones*, please." With treats in hand, Mary Jane followed Ernie's sister, Debbie, into the foldout rumble seat in the back of the hot rod. Ernie's '32 rumbled for a minute then took off up the street much slower than usual.

"Wow! Mary Jane is riding in Ernie's car," I said out loud and looked for Pete.

"I need a washcloth," said Gail as she tugged on my sleeve

with goopy fingers.

"Get me one, too," whined Kathleen as she wiped melted ice cream on her T-shirt.

Good thing I changed my clothes after school. The kids made my printed shirt a sticky mess with their sticky fingers. *Oops, a piece of* Strawberry Shortcake *bar plopped onto my shirt.* I licked it off. *Yum. Glad I beat Hey Pup to it.*

"Okay, kids. Let's go into the house, so Granny Mary can clean you up," I said.

Back on our blanket, I kneeled down to work on my scrapbook. The kids dug into a box of dress-up clothes. Hey Pup dragged a scrap of fabric around. He growled, and sniffed, and pounced on it every other second. His wagging tail beat at the air.

Next to the street, a giant walnut tree waved in the breeze creating patterns of light and shadow across the yard. Hey Pup left his fabric scrap to chase shadows. He pounced on them, too. That same breeze blew over some chicken smells to my nose. *Yuck. Does Mr. Chester ever get an ice cream, I wondered? Does he miss his puppy?*

The kids squabbled over outfits, so they could play Peter Pan like the TV play.

"I wanna be Wendy, so I need the blue dress," said Mandy. "Blue matches my eyes."

"I wanna be Peter Pan," said Kathleen. "Charlie, you play Captain Hook."

"No, I wanna be the crocodile," said Little Charlie.

"Hey, Carol Ann, why are you kneeling?" Pete asked as he sat down. "Are you praying out here in your yard? We kneel down at our church. Some of my friends think that's un-cool. Does God hear us better when we're on our knees?"

"I think God likes to hear from us wherever we are," I said. "Maybe we're more tuned in to Him on our knees. Don't ever feel un-cool about praying."

"So, are you praying?" asked Pete.

"No, I'm working on a project," I said. "I'm making a scrapbook about my dad and me and the famous people he's met. It's called *Harry Hartnell's Famous Faces*."

"That's cool," said Pete as he wiggled the puppy's fabric scrap and teased him. "Hey Pup, this is my material."

Hey Pup left his shadow chasing to do some fabric chasing instead. His sharp teeth chomped down on the material that Pete wiggled. The puppy growled playfully, shook his head, bounced like a ball, and never let go of his fabric prize. Pete pulled the scrap with one hand and opened my scrapbook with the other hand.

"Who's in it?" Pete asked as he opened it. "Hey, there are only two pictures in here: a Civil War soldier and Joe DiMaggio, my favorite baseball player."

"I'm putting more stuff in it today," I said, and looked at the puppy's foot on the page. I moved the small white paw. "Hey Pup, your paw is not the *stuff* I'm talking about. I'm putting some family pictures in it and movie stars that Dad met. These are their paper dolls."

Pete said, "So tell me about these two guys and their stuff."

"As a boy, Dad lived in Chicago, Illinois," I said. "One day a Civil War soldier, dressed in a uniform, visited my dad's first-grade classroom. The soldier told Dad's class about the Civil War. Dad never forgot that visit. Then when Dad turned eleven or twelve, he got an autograph from Joe DiMaggio at Comiskey Park, Chicago's baseball field."

"Like wow!" Pete said. He flipped several pages. "Where

is it? Where's the autograph of one of the best baseball players to ever swing a bat?"

"Well…my dad and his friends ran down the sidewalk and threw Joe DiMaggio's autograph in the street. They didn't know its future value." I shrugged.

"That's bad news," said a disappointed Pete. "I wanted to see DiMaggio's autograph. Who are these movie star paper dolls? Are they going into your scrapbook?"

"Yes, they are." I held up a page with Susan Hayward on it. She stood next to a gorgeous, long, red sparkly dress. "You use the scissors to cut around the small tabs on her dress. Then you cut out Susan Hayward. She wore this dress in a movie called *With a Song in My Heart*. Do you want to cut these out?"

Pete shook his head. "No. I'd cut out a cowboy paper doll, but I'm not cutting out that fancy actress and her fancy clothes," said Pete as a commotion began behind us.

"I'm Captain Hook. I said to walk the plank!" Little Charlie yelled at Mandy, who had dressed up as Wendy. *Woof, woof,* barked the puppy at mean, old Captain Hook.

"Never, Captain Hook," yelled Kathleen, dressed as Peter Pan. Then in a sweet voice she said some words from the play, "Think lovely thoughts, Wendy, so you can fly away."

All the kids, in their crazy costumes, ran around the ivy-covered posts on the front porch while Captain Hook and Hey Pup chased them. They circled the blanket and fell down laughing. Cathie got tangled up in her great grandma's opera cape. The pup circled, too, then dropped down panting. His pink tongue hung out like an extra floppy ear.

"Can I play Peter Pan since my name's Peter?" Pete asked as he jumped up and waved his arms in the air. "See, I can fly.

'I'll teach you how to jump on the wind's back'. I love that line from the play."

Gail popped up. She said, "No, silly. Kathleen's Peter Pan and I'm a Last Boy."

"I think you mean *Lost* Boy," Pete said. "You got lost and Peter found you."

I said, "We watched *Peter Pan* last month on TV. They've played it ever since."

"Yeah, we watched it too. I liked the flying stuff." Pete spread his arms again to mimic flying. "My mom heard that sixty-five million people watched the play on TV."

"Wow!" I said. "I loved Mary Martin as Peter Pan. She looked like a boy."

"That stunk. A girl pretending to be Peter Pan was a dumb idea," said Pete.

"The story of Peter Pan is like real life," I said. "Kids want to escape to a place like Neverland. In Neverland, you could play forever and never grow up. But even there, dangers lurked everywhere. Everyone ran from the Indians, the Pirates, Captain Hook, and the crocodile that swallowed the clock."

"Tic, toc, tic, toc," ticked Pete. "In the play, the crocodile looked cool as he crawled on his belly chasing Captain Hook. This summer I wanna escape to that new amusement park in Anaheim when it opens. I'll go on wild rides, eat popcorn, fight bad guys, and pretend that I'll never grow up. I'm Peter…Pan…Hawking, ya know."

Captain Hook ran by yelling, "See, he's licking his lips for the rest of me." Hey Pup chased Captain Hook across the porch. The puppy didn't look much like a crocodile, though.

Pete looked at Little Charlie who doubled as Captain

Hook. "Hey, stop a minute, kid. You've got a great belt buckle, Little Charlie. Where'd you get it?"

Little Charlie stopped to rub the shiny buckle. The puppy stopped to rub his nose on his paw. My cousin said, "I got my Buffalo Bob belt and buckle for twenty-five cents plus three candy bar wrappers. My mom helped me send them in. This came in the mail."

"Good choice, kid," said Pete. "That's the buckle Captain Hook *would* wear." Pete looked down at me and said, "Get up, Carol Ann. I've got a fun idea. Let's dress Hey Pup up as the crocodile with a ticking clock and everything."

I stood up, brushed myself off, and said, "Okay. I get first dibs on the costumes."

While I kneeled down next to the costume box, Pete ran in circles with Hey Pup. I pulled out a strip of green fabric, some green ribbon, and a cardboard clock. This would work for Hey Pup's crocodile suit. I stepped into a brown, fringed skirt. Then I slipped a matching fringed top over my head. This costume covered my clothes and turned me into an Indian princess. I draped a handful of colorful bead necklaces around my neck.

"Okay, Pete," I said, "there's lots of cool pirate stuff in the box for you." Hey Pup bounced over to me and wiggled as I wrapped him up. He nipped at the green ribbons I used to tie on the green fabric. I put a cardboard clock on a ribbon and tied it around the pup's neck. When I let him go he ran in circles trying to shed his green crocodile "skin."

"How do you like my costume?" Pete asked me. "What do you think, puppy?"

"I think you look like a clown pirate," I said. "Look pup, doesn't Pete look like a clown with those polka dot pants and that fringe around his neck?"

"Call me the Polka Dot Pirate," laughed Pete. "Hey kids, can we join you?"

Pete, Hey Pup, and I ran with the kids across the yard, across the porch, and up and down the driveway. Screaming kids ran from Hey Pup the Crocodile. Captain Hook stopped to let Hey Pup lick his face. Then all the kids bent down to tickle and pet the pup.

We joined the kids as they ran around singing, "I won't grow up, I don't wanna wear a tie…I'll never grow up, never grow up, never grow u…up, not I."

I dropped on the blanket and said, "The princess is pooped…I'm a party-pooper."

"I'm done, too. Are you watching these ankle-biters?" Pete asked as Crocodile Pup playfully bit his ankle. "Pup you're supposed to bite Captain Hook, not his pirate."

"You're such a silly puppy," I said. "Go find the captain." Hey Pup scampered over to chase the kids. "I'm helping Granny Mary by keeping the kids out of the street while I wait for the mailman. Aunt Ruthie's expecting an important package."

"I'll help you," said Pete. "I'm waiting for a record to arrive in the mail."

"You'd better change out of your pirate, clown costume before the neighbors see you and wonder what circus is in town," I said. "I wish I had a camera."

"I'm changing, I'm changing," Pete said as he slipped out of his polka dots and clown collar.

"Did you get to watch the *Lone Ranger* on TV last night?" I asked Pete.

"I did. 'Hi, Ho Silver and the Lone Ranger rides again.'

What a hoss show."

"Will you watch *Rin Tin Tin* tonight at 7:30?" I asked. "He's the coolest dog. He could teach Hey Pup some tricks. Could the puppy learn tricks from watching TV?"

"I don't think so, but I wish he could," said Pete. "It's Friday night at the black and white television set. My dad loves *Rin Tin Tin, Ozzie and Harriet*, and *Ray Bolger*. I'll ask Mom to pop some corn." Pete rubbed a circle on his stomach. "I only wish I had a plate of your mom's cookies, and a playful pup to bark at the bad guys."

The roadside gravel crunched as the mailman slowly drove up and stopped. The mailman stepped out of his mail truck. He walked into our yard and pulled a package from his mail sack. "Hello, kids," he said. "Is Dr. Ruth McCammon here?"

"No, she's at work," I said as I jumped up and brushed off my fringed skirt. The kids stopped running, so they could see the new character in our Neverland.

"I've got an important package for Dr. Ruth McCammon. Could you give it to her, please?" asked the mailman.

"Yes, I will," I told him. "I'll take it into the house." The mailman handed me the package. I hurried past the kids and into Aunt Ruthie's house. The sender had addressed the package to Dr. Ruth McCammon, 5659 La Madera Avenue, El Monte, California. On the right corner of the package, a postmark stamped the date, April 20, 1955. The return address read Cutter Laboratories, Berkeley, California.

The screen door slammed behind me. I dodged Captain Hook, Crocodile Pup, Peter Pan, Wendy, the Lost Boy, and Cathie as Tiger Lily in her embroidered cape. Back on the blanket, I set down a box of doggie treats. Crocodile Pup bounced to the blanket.

I held up a bone-shaped treat and said, "Sit." He looked at me, wagged his tail, and sat down. "Here's your treat, you smart little crocodile cutie."

When the kids leaned back and forth in a dance, I jumped up and leaned back and forth, too. We bent over and bounce-stepped around the porch singing as a group, "Ugga, wugga, wig-wam. Ugga, wugga, wig-wam." My beads bounced and clicked with each step.

"You're Neverland Indians now," said Pete. "Where'd Hook and the Croc go?"

"To the monkey bars," I told Pete as I looked back at the house. "I hope Aunt Ruthie's package doesn't have anything scary in it like a shot. Yikes. A laboratory in northern California shipped that package to my aunt."

"You snooped at your aunt's mail," said Pete.

"I didn't snoop at it. The address stared at me when I took the package into the house. Besides, *you* get the prize for snooping. You snooped on Mr. Chester then you made us stay there with you," I said and cringed.

"Yeah, Mary Jane didn't like the spots from our snooping," said Pete.

I said, "My mom wanted to call Aunt Ruthie when I walked through the door all spotty. I washed off the blood to show her I was okay."

"My mom says your aunt is special," said Pete. "The other day, Mom defended your aunt at the grocery store. I went with Mom to help out. We heard ladies gossiping about your aunt. Mom told them your aunt is a talented doctor and a wonderful wife, mother, neighbor, and friend. Unlike them, Dr. Ruth McCammon uses her time productively instead of gossiping in the grocery store."

"Wow. Your mom's brave to stick up like that for Aunt Ruthie," I said.

"Any time, Carol Ann," Pete said. "My mom likes your family."

"I wish I could be brave like your mom and courageous like my aunt. She had the courage to work at a job during high school, to go to medical school, to become a doctor, to have babies, to work outside her home on scary stuff in a laboratory, to ignore gossip about having a man's job, *and* to drive a car."

"You have courage like that, Carol Ann," Pete said. "You could grow up to be a doctor just like your aunt Ruthie or a mom who raises some kids like you and me."

"I don't think I could be a doctor, but I'd like being a mom," I said.

"Someday you could go to college, or drive a car, or write a book. You're a kid, but you bravely stood up to Mr. Chester to say, 'Sorry.' Doing that took a whole bunch of courage," said Pete.

"Was that courage?" I asked. "I showed him manners and the royal law."

"My dad says courage means to face danger bravely," Pete said. "You did."

"Thanks, Pete, but I didn't feel very brave. I felt scared."

"Then you're a scared kid like the rest of us. Luckily, you've got lots of cool heroes like your aunt, John Wayne, and me," said Pete with a grin.

I bent over and picked up Hey Pup and said, "I'm gonna need a load of courage when this guy gets too big to crawl under our fence, or Mr. Chester ties him up for escaping all the time. I'll miss him running in our yard and doing tricks for doggie treats. I'll miss his puppy licks, too. I wish he belonged to me."

Just then the Peter Pan and Captain Hook bunch ran back to circle around us. Mandy, dressed as Wendy, cried, "You're our hero, Peter Pan."

Pete laughed at them. He said, "See, even Wendy and the Lost Boy have a hero."

"I wanna be the hero next time!" yelled Captain Hook.

"I wanna be Princess Tiger Lily again," said cousin Cathie as she pushed back her cape.

ROARRRRRRRRRRRRRRR, RUMBLE, RUM, RUM. POP.

Ernie's black, 1932 Ford Hi-boy screeched to a stop in Pete's driveway. The Ford V8 engine idled loudly. Ernie, Hawk, and Tim liked tinkering with the engine to speed it up.

Mary Jane and Debbie bobbed around in the rumble seat and sang along with the song, "Earth Angel," by The Penguins. Every time Ernie revved the hot rod's engine, I smelled exhaust fumes. Hawk climbed out of the car, looked at us, and nodded.

Hawk said to Ernie, "Don't split, I need something from my car." Ernie gunned the engine and turned up the radio. The hot rod rumbled and rattled like a caged animal.

Pete whispered, "Mom said Mary Jane could ride with Debbie in her brother's car if Ernie drove slowly and carefully. That'll be really tough for him. He likes speed."

"I hope Ernie listens to your mom," I whispered back.

Aunt Ruthie drove past Ernie's '32 and into our driveway. She opened her car's heavy door and stepped out holding an armload of papers, a jacket, and a pretty purse.

"You got a package, Aunt Ruthie," I said. "I carried it into the house for you."

"Thank you, Carol Ann." She shifted her stuff to one arm as she straightened her dark, gray skirt. As always, she looked glamorous in a white blouse and simple straight skirt, belted at the waist. Her high heels clicked on the driveway. *Click, click, click.* She disappeared into the house. The screen door slammed shut.

"Pete...eeeeeee!" Mary Jane called.

Pete walked over to Ernie's '32 and asked, "What do you want?"

"Debbie and I want to take the puppy for a short ride," she said. "We want to see his floppy ears waving in the wind."

"Hey Pup can't ride in Ernie's car," Pete said and looked at me. "He's not our puppy. If you want him to go for a ride, you'll have to talk to Mr. Chester."

"Never mind," said Mary Jane. "I didn't want pup slobber all over me anyway."

RUMBLE, RUM, RUM. Ernie gunned the hot rod then combed his goopy hair.

"He'd better not cut out 'til Hawk gets back," said Pete. "Ernie's so impatient."

Just then, Ernie gunned the engine one final time, backed out of the driveway, and punched it. He roared down the street in his powerful machine.

SQUEEEEEEEEALLL, CRAAAAAASSSSSSSH, CRUU-UUUUNNNNNCH.

We looked down the street to see a pile of steaming wreckage. *Yikes!* Ernie's radio blasted out the tune, "Ain't That A Shame," by Fats Domino. The two girls were screaming. Crushed metal lay in twisted piles on the oil-drenched road.

Pete yelled in a shaky voice, "Tell Dr. Ruth that Ernie's had an awful accident and to hurry!" He sprinted flat out to the crashed car and his screaming sister.

The crash ended our front yard fun. Before I could even take two steps toward the house, Aunt Ruthie ran out through the screen door. She gripped a black medical bag. Her beautiful face had a worried look on it.

"Keep the kids in the yard, Carol Ann," Aunt Ruthie called over her shoulder. She hurried onto La Madera Avenue toward Ernie's crashed car. Hawk rushed his mom down their driveway and then down the neighbor-filled street.

Crying *Peter Pan* players crowded around me. Cathie snuggled into her opera cape. Hey Pup snuggled into my shoulder. He whimpered like he knew something was wrong. None of us were in Neverland anymore…this was very real.

"Everything will be okay, kids," I said. "Let's pray. O God, give Pete's mom your courage. O God, help Aunt Ruthie to help Ernie, Debbie, and Mary Jane." I wiped my tear-stained face with a shaky hand. "Thank you, God, that Tim, Hawk, Pete, and Hey Pup weren't in Ernie's hot rod, too. Amen."

Wooooooooooooooooo!   We-ah!   We-ah!   We-ah! Woooooooooooooooooooo!

An ambulance wailed its message of help and hope in the distance. *Is it arriving too late? Will something in Aunt Ruthie's package be able to help?*

Ahwoooooooooooooooooooooooo! Hey Pup howled along with the approaching ambulance. He seemed to say things were really bad.

Chapter Eleven

The Birthday Party

▼▲▼▲▼▲▼▲▼▲▼▲▼▲▼▲▼▲▼▲▼▲▼▲▼▲

Da dump, da dump, da dump.

My head pounded to the beat of my heart. This headache started early this morning. *Am I getting a cold? Not until after the party, please.* My face looked normal in the bathroom mirror. I tucked my hair behind my ear.

"Did you find the aspirin, Carol Ann?" Mom called from the kitchen.

"Yes, I see it in the medicine cabinet between the seltzer tablets and the dry skin cream," I said. I reached a shaky hand into the medicine cabinet to get an aspirin.

"Take one with a glass of water," Mom said. "Stay home if you're sick."

"I'm fine. I have a tiny headache," I said. My scratchy throat swallowed the aspirin. *Gulp, gulp, gulp.* I shivered, sniffed, and felt my cold forehead. A stuffy nose and stiff neck seemed to be the problem. I'd feel better in a little while.

I fluffed the skirt on my lacy aqua-blue dress. Then I picked up the pretty present and the pink invitation that said:

PLEASE JOIN US

FOR: Mary Jane's Birthday Party
DATE: April 24, 1955
TIME: 2:00 P.M. - 5:00 P.M.
PLACE: The Hawking's Residence
5657 La Madera Avenue, El Monte

Mary Jane's present rested in the bend of my arm. Last night Aunt Ruthie helped me wrap the present in pink rose-bud paper. We tied a pretty, pink bow on it to hold down a signed and sealed "happy birthday" card. My shoes left prints on Uncle Charlie's freshly mowed grass as I crossed to Mary Jane's birthday bash.

Pete whistled from his yard and said, "Boss-looking gift, Carol Ann. Glad you could make the scene." He looked cool in his threads. He shook his head as he looked behind me and smiled.

"Hey, look who wants to crash the party," said Pete. "Hey Pup is on your heels."

I turned my pounding head on my stiff neck to see the puppy waiting patiently to follow me through the open gate and into Pete's yard. This playful pup would pester starched petticoats, presents, and dressed-up party guests.

"I'm sorry, pup, but you're stuck in my yard today," I said. "And no digging."

Pete said, "If he digs under the gate, I'll take him back to his home."

"Thanks, Pete," I said as I squeezed through the gate. "Hey Pup scrunched down with his head on his paws. Then he sniffed, twisted his head, sighed, and waited.

Partygoers gushed into Pete's backyard. Boys dressed in suits walked next to girls in pastel, printed, puff-sleeved, full-skirted dresses fluffed over starched petticoats. Each kid cradled a present like an official offering.

Mary Jane looked like a princess in pink, polka-dot chiffon. Stiff petticoats rustled under a full skirt. She accepted each gift personally, royally, and willingly.

"Thank you for coming," she said.

"What a gorgeous gift. For me?" she asked.

"So nice to see you," she complimented.

"I'm fine, thank you. I'll get the cast off in six weeks," she answered.

"Yes, I'm lucky to be alive. I only have a broken arm and a black eye," she said.

"What lovely wrapping paper," she gushed.

"We spent one night in the hospital," she explained.

"Thank you for coming," she said.

I handed her my gift. She took it, shook it, and whispered through a snarling smile, "This better be good."

"Carol Ann, we've got dibs on that back table over there," Pete motioned for me to follow him. I wiggled my stiff shoulders and followed him. "Sit here, next to Mandy. You can enjoy the party with us."

"Thanks, Pete," I said as I sat down and rubbed my stiff neck.

The backyard looked like a pink paradise. Tables, dressed

in flowing pink tablecloths, had been arranged on the lawn. Pink paper plates and napkins circled each tabletop. Pink crepe paper and balloons draped the tree branches. Rosebud centerpieces decorated each table. The roses smelled heavenly. Everything looked so beautiful.

I looked around and said, "Wow, Pete, what a perfect Hollywood-type party."

Pete grumbled, "The party cost as much as a Hollywood party. Mary Jane gets whatever Mary Jane wants," Pete spread his arms. "She wanted all this."

Mandy chirped, "Hawk said she's spoiled."

I rubbed the top of my tingling leg. I said, "Everyone deserves to be spoiled on their special day, don't they?" I pushed down my cramped foot.

Pete said, "Yeah, but she thinks every day is her special day."

Mandy shook her head up and down, "Yeah."

I shivered. "Spoiled or not, I'm having a blast," I lied and shivered some more.

Pete frowned. "Are you feeling okay?"

"Maybe I'm getting a tiny cold," I said and sniffed my stuffy nose. Then I took a gulp of pink lemonade to soothe my sore throat.

Mary Jane's group created a commotion at her special table. She looked like royalty sitting in spoiled splendor on a chair decked out in pink balloons. Her chair looked like a puffy, pink throne. Mary Jane's curly blonde up-do needed a sparkling tiara.

Frank Sinatra crooned from the radio, "I've Got The World On A String."

Ahwoooooooooooooooo, crooned Hey Pup from my backyard.

I glanced over at the gate where I left him. The puppy stuck a paw through the fence.

"My pink world is so positively perfect except for that howling puppy," Mary Jane gushed as she clapped her cast. "Can someone please make that dog stop howling? He's spoiling my party."

Pete whispered, "She'll spoil her own party with her howling. The puppy won't. She thinks she's "Queen For A Day" – today and everyday."

I nudged him. She deserved to be a queen today, or a princess anyway. I liked her perfect party, but I felt perfectly horrible. I wiped my sweaty neck. *Why do I feel so hot? I hope I'm not getting Jimmie's sickness!*

Good thing my heat wave didn't melt the cake. Three graduating layers of pink, culinary confection described the cake. Small, pink plates plus a bouquet of rosebuds shared the tablecloth on the cake table. Thirteen candles circled the top of the cake like a crown.

"I hope Mary Jane cuts her cake, soon," said Mandy as she licked her lips.

"I'm glad Mary Jane's okay and that the crash didn't cancel her party," I said as I patted my sour stomach. My head pulsed in pain, but I smiled anyway like a Hollywood actress. I had a job to do. I must act like a kid having a good time.

Pete answered, "The heat, I mean police, said Mary Jane was a lucky girl to survive the accident. I got scared at the crash until I saw Mary Jane squawking and struggling to get outta Ernie's wrecked car. She looked like one of Mr. Chester's chickens. Hey Pup would have sniffed at her then howled."

I laughed and asked, "Is Ernie in trouble for driving too fast and crashing?"

Pete pointed up the driveway. "Ask him yourself. He's next to Hawk's car."

BRUMMM, BRUMMM, BRUMMM roared the engine of Hawk's Ride. The classic car waited on the driveway. "Ernie, watch out for the paint job," warned Hawk.

Ernie rode on a beat-up bicycle. His head was bandaged. He looked over at us then quickly looked away. *Is he embarrassed to now be riding a bike like us kids ride?* Hawk's recently restored 1937 Ford Slant back looked beautiful. Painted flames, like wings, licked along the shimmering red-orange paint job on the car's steel sides. The Ford's chrome trim, headlights, and grill glistened.

Ernie parked his bike and got into Hawk's car. He said, "Let's split, Hawk."

Hawk waved from his flame-painted Ford and said, "Happy birthday, sis."

BRUMMM, BRUMMM, roared Hawk's Ride as it backed up the driveway.

Pete watched them go. "Hawk's Ford is so cool. Now Hawk drives Ernie around. Since the crash, Ernie's grounded forever. Ernie's dad got really frosted."

"Listen up everyone," said Mary Jane. She pounded her cast on the table. "Let's play some games, eat cake with ice cream, then I'll open my presents."

"Let's walk around, Carol Ann," said Pete. "You're looking as pink as the party."

I felt pink like the party, with my pulsing head, achy knees, stiff neck, and sore throat. Kids lined up for the game called "Pin The Tail On The Donkey." Mary Jane ordered a kid to turn up Hawk's radio for Musical Chairs. "Mambo Italiano" by Rosemary Clooney got all the kids jumping with excitement.

When the music stopped, kids rushed to sit down. One unlucky girl had no chair. Debbie was the unlucky girl. She tumbled to the ground in a swirl of petticoats. Bandages covered cuts and scrapes on her face, arms, hands, and knees. Debbie had survived the crash of her brother's '32 Ford with minor injuries. At just that moment a dirt-covered puppy bounded over to Debbie to attack her kicking feet. Pete laughed at that.

I quickly scooped up the pup. With him on my shoulder and a party favor in my shaky hand, I stepped past the birthday cake. Hey Pup sniffed the sugary, sweet air. "I'm checking out the presents," I lied to Pete who had lined up to play "Pin The Tail On The Donkey." My pretty present for Mary Jane sat on the gift table.

"Put the puppy down and get in line!" Pete shouted to me before a blindfold covered his eyes. "Hey, where'd the party go?"

I left the party and escaped through the gate into my yard. My legs wobbled with every step. I carefully carried Hey Pup so I wouldn't drop him. *What's wrong with me? Did I finally get Jimmie's yucky strep throat? Yikes. That means some of Aunt Ruthie's yucky medicine and her shot pot!*

I walked past my porch toward our back fence. "I'm so sorry, puppy, but you have to go home. I don't feel well so I can't play with you today. Be a good puppy and chase some chickens in your own yard." I put the pup down and gently pushed him under the fence. He whimpered when I mounded dirt and a large rock over his escape hole.

"You belong to Mr. Chester, and you need to stay in his yard," I sniffed back some tears. "No one is home today, and

I'm afraid you'll get hurt, so stay away. I love you, but you don't belong to me and you never will."

Several chickens charged by me as I walked across the grass. Mr. Chester's dogs barked as I stepped onto my porch. My family wasn't home, so only silence greeted me. I dropped my shoes next to my bed. I climbed under the covers. I heard a faint *woof, woof, woof, awhoooooooooooooo.*

"*Awwwwwwwwww,*" I sighed.

The sheets cooled my feverish body. A party sound, "Sh-Boom, Sh-Boom, life could be a dream," floated in the window as I drifted down, down, down into my own delirious dream. A crazy kaleidoscope of colors and dream scenes danced in my pounding head like a movie.

RUMBLE, RUM, RUM roared Ernie's wrecked car as it drove along the road with a bicycle strapped to it. Hawk's flame-covered Ford followed close behind it.

"I can beat you, Carol Ann, if I punch it!" Ernie yelled at me then raced his wrecked car around the corner.

I hurried up the road toward Cherrylee School. I clutched a birthday present under one arm and Hey Pup under the other. Becky, Eileen, and Susan hurried past me with the Easter Parade.

"Sorry you're sick," called Becky. "I hope you don't have polio."

What were the polio symptoms Mom listed that day in her kitchen? I tried to remember. Oh, yeah. The list included a sore throat, a fever, and a stiff neck. Yikes. And didn't she say that puppies couldn't get polio?

In the cafetorium, pink decorations draped everything. Pink balloons hung from the rafters like goopy globs of already-been-chewed bubblegum. Mary Jane sat like a queen on her pink bubblegum throne. She wore a dress made from yards of pink chiffon.

"I'm Queen For Today and everyone in this zoo better bow to me," she said. "This is my Atomic Cafetorium!"

Every time she pounded her cast, an atom bomb flashed and spiraled up into a mushroom cloud. I ducked onto the floor then covered my neck. Hey Pup snuggled next to me and sniffed the air.

"In Las Vegas, people watch the blast from the comfort of their favorite casino," crowed Mr. Chicken-Headed Chester. Growling dogs crowded his crippled legs. "Hey Pup, is that you hiding down there? You get over here right now! You belong to me!"

Hey Pup lifted his head and growled at Mr. Chicken-Headed Chester. He didn't move, and I didn't make him. "Stay with me, pup, so I can protect you," I said as I stood up with him still safe under my arm.

Miss East sang, "Jesus loves you this I know for the Bible tells me so."

Party guests gathered around Mary Jane: the ice cream man, Miss Nelson and her blackboard, Granny Mary holding snotty-nosed Jimmie, Betsy McCall, Peter Pan, Captain Hook, Mr. Potato Head, Dr. Jonas Salk, Hawk, Ernie on his bicycle, Tim leaning on his crutches, and the clock-swallowing crocodile looking for a tasty treat.

Mr. Chicken-Headed Chester rolled out a ten-tiered birthday cake covered in glowing candles. Their heat fried me. I wiped my feverish forehead.

Everyone started singing, "Happy birthday to you, happy birthday to you, happy birthday, Mary Jane, happy birthday to you." Ahwoooooooooooo!

"Stop that howling, you hound dog. Have a piece of cake, Carol Ann. You didn't have any at my other party," said Mary Jane. She cut into the pink, frosted confection. Out of the soft, white cake oozed chicken blood like red, wiggly worms. Yikes.

"I'll have some later," I said politely before I snuck away.

I heard heavy breathing behind me. Coffin-like iron lungs held living children struggling to breathe. In and out they sucked air. The polio poster, from downtown El Monte, came to life. A girl limped toward me on legs encased in metal braces.

She pointed her crutch at me and said, "Fight polio. Join the March of Dimes. Put your dimes in the red and white can at your school. Please help me." Her face started changing until she looked like…me.

"I helped you," I cried out. "I did put my dimes into the can at school."

Super-sized syringes and pointy needles danced around her to the tune of "Shake, Rattle, and Roll" by Bill Haley and His Comets. Polio Pioneers bravely rolled up their sleeves to get ready for Dr. Salk's polio vaccine. I didn't want the sting of Dr. Salk's brand new polio vaccine. Yikes. O God, help me to be brave. I need courage.

"Pete said a shot was just a sting," I remembered.

Massive marbles rolled around the cafetorium. A cat's-eye marble whooshed past me. My friends played foursquare until the ball rolled away. The ball fell into a mud hole that grew into a giant muddy mouth that tried to swallow us. Was there polio in the mud? Woof, woof, woof.

Mr. Bailey waved his belt as he chased his boys. He yelled, "I told you not to build a fallout shelter in my yard."

"Oh, Mr. Bailey, it'll save us from Mary Jane's atom bombs," I pleaded.

"Nothing can save you from them," Mary Jane cackled. "I'm the Queen of the Atomic Cafetorium, so I control the bombs. Have some delicious birthday cake. And give me that puppy. It's my party, and I want that puppy!"

The mailman munched on a cookie, as his shoe crunched an Easter egg. He held out a package. 'From Cutter Laboratories' beamed brightly on the box in neon letters. What scary thing lurked in that box? Would that scary thing go into Aunt Ruthie's shot pot? If it did, I wish Aunt Ruthie had never gotten her package in Neverland during this scary spring!

"I didn't mean to snoop at it, Pete. I couldn't look away. I'm sorry." I said.

"Grab that party-pooper," ordered Mary Jane. She pointed to me.

Giant, glowing candles glided towards me on wax puddle feet. Their waxy arms grabbed at me.

"Help me!" I shouted. "She's trying to take my puppy!"

"This way," an angel called to me as he waved his glowing arm. A felt tomb stood behind him. Brown felt rocks surrounded the cave-like tomb. From the top of the felt cave, The Old Rugged Cross shed a saving shadow.

"No one leaves my party," shouted Mary Jane. "Give me that puppy!"

The angel said to me, "Don't be afraid, He is risen."

"Carol Ann, where are you?" Pete called desperately from inside the tomb.

I turned to the party guests. "I'm sorry, Mr. Chester, that you have yucky chicken poop on your boots. Enjoy your wormy cake, Mary Jane. Bye, everyone," I said before running into the cave. The felty darkness enclosed me. My arms felt empty. Oh no! I left Hey Pup behind! Hey Pup is lost! I clawed my way to freedom.

Mary Jane's laughing voice echoed behind me, "April Fools."

"Carol Ann," Pete's frantic voice said. "You're real sick."

I pushed my way out of my blankets. My eyes squinted and blinked. I licked my cracked lips then swallowed. "I'm thirsty," I croaked then weakly kicked at the rest of my blankets. They piled into a fabric puddle on the floor.

"I'm here, Carol Ann, and I'll get you some water," said a muffled voice that sounded like Pete's voice only different.

I patted my sheet. "Where's Hey Pup?" I cried out. "I lost him in the cave! Help him, please. Someone help him!" I looked up at Pete.

He looked funny with a mask over his lower face. "I'll help him, Carol Ann, but first drink something." He helped me sip some liquid. "You scared us. You disappeared from the birthday party. When your parents got home they couldn't find you, so I started the search. We found you hiding under your covers. Man, you're burning up."

"Thank you for leading our search party, Pete," said Aunt Ruthie. "Carol Ann's a very sick girl. Let me check her, again, and keep that mask on." My mom hovered over my aunt's shoulder. Mom's scared eyes blinked above her own white hospital mask.

Dr. Ruth McCammon prodded and poked me in her most professional manner. She took a thermometer out of my mouth. Her eyebrows waved up when she read it. She pulled scary instruments from her black medical bag. Aunt Ruthie checked my throat, my eyes, my nose, my ears, and my chest. She tapped, tapped, tapped on my legs in her most gentle manner.

"You'll be all right," Mom said in a muffled voice.

"You'll have a tale to tell, nightingale," said Pete through his mask, "Especially with your nest of a hairdo. Hey Pup would howl at your "do" and want to pounce on it. Then he would sniff, sniff, sniff."

Aunt Ruthie's voice whispered from the doorway. She said,

"The thermometer read 103 degrees. We've got to bring her fever down. Let's bathe her in cool washcloths, so she won't go into convulsions. I've got some special medicine for her."

"What's wrong with her, Ruthie? Does she have polio?" Mom asked in a whisper.

"I don't know, Jeanne. She's got polio symptoms, but let's not jump to wrong conclusions. We'll bring her fever down and watch her for twenty-four hours. If she doesn't improve, we'll call an ambulance service. They will take her to the Sister Elizabeth Kenny Polio Hospital out on Gillman Road."

I nodded off for a minute then shivered awake. I smelled alcohol. *Yikes. That's the smell before a shot. Be brave, Carol Ann.* A cool cloth swiped my feverish forehead. I flipped back and forth from sizzling hot to freezing cold. When Mom poured cherry-flavored syrup down my swollen throat, I gagged but kept it down.

Sniffle, sniffle, sniffle, sniffed my crying sisters from the doorway.

"Please watch her, Pete," Mom said.

"No sweat, Mrs. H." Pete turned to me. He said through his mask, "Go ahead and pile up some Z's, Carol Ann. You've got courage to fight this scary sickness. You're brave. Stop worrying and remember your heroes."

Pete's words swam around in my head. "Have courage." "Don't die." "You can take a shot." "Don't be afraid." That's what the angel said before I ran into the brown felt cave. That's where I lost Hey Pup!

I felt afraid then I felt the bed sag down. What was that? My tired eyes cracked open then closed. I opened them again and worked extra hard to focus.

Pete kneeled next to my bed. He pressed his hands together and bowed his head. "Dear, God, I don't know much about praying. I'm on my knees, so you can hear me better. Please help Carol Ann and make her well. Give her courage, if she needs a shot. Give Dr. Ruth wisdom to take care of her. Please, don't let Carol Ann die. Thanks God," he prayed in a muffled, choked-up voice.

I stared at him through eye-slits. "Good prayer," I croaked like a frog. "Thanks."

Pete said through his mask, "Maybe you won't need a shot. But if you do, remember a shot's just a little sting. I'd take it for you if I could. I'd role up my sleeve, relax, and POW! The sting would be over in a second. Getting a shot beats giving a speech in front of our class at Cherrylee School. Facing Mr. Chester, like you did, took more courage than getting a scary shot."

Aunt Ruthie walked into the room carrying a familiar looking package. "Time to go, Pete. You can visit our girl to-morrow. Hopefully, she'll be better in the morning."

Pete's muffled voice said, "Don't worry, Carol Ann. Dr. Ruth took good care of Mary Jane. She'll take good care of you, too. She'll be very gentle. By the way, I saved you some birthday cake from the birthday party. See ya later, alligator."

"After while, crocodile," I growled through the gunk in my throat.

Aunt Ruthie said, "Carol Ann, I received some medicine from Cutter Laboratories that will make you well."

She set the Cutter Laboratories box down on my night-stand. *Do the letters have a faint neon glow? Does the box contain the polio vaccine?*

Outside my room, Dad asked, "Does she have polio? Will she be crippled?"

Screech, screech, screech, floated through my open window on a faint breeze that smelled like chicken poop. The lifted curtains waved like ghostly arms. *Ahwoooooooooo,* wafted through the window. *What is that scary sound?*

I shivered. My head hurt. My legs felt numb. I needed my aunt's medicine, so I wouldn't get polio. The fever swallowed me up. *Is this how Mr. Chester felt all those years ago? No shot is as bad as getting polio and Mr. Chester's crippled legs and heart.*

I needed a nice Neverland to escape to for safety. I hurt all over. *O God, help me, please,* I prayed. A Bible verse echoed in my mind. *Psalm 4:8 said, 'I will both lay me down in peace and sleep: for Thou, Lord, makest me to dwell in safety.'* My quiet room surrounded me as I drifted down a dark, dream-like road.

"Carol Ann," Aunt Ruthie said as she gently shook my shoulder. "Are you ready for the medicine that will make you feel better?"

Even in my dreamy state, that sentence sounded familiar. *Yikes. That's what Aunt Ruthie said before she gave cousin Jimmie a shot. I hate shots. They sting, and they're soooooo scary. But I need one or I'll die because I'm so sick.*

I feel so sick, I just want to sleep and never wake up. But who would tease Pete if I'm gone? Who would help Mom with the kids? Who would watch out for Hey Pup when he escapes into our yard? Who would pray for Mr. Chester?

"You can give me your medicine, Aunt Ruthie. I want to get well," I whispered.

I swallowed another lump of gunk in my throat. I prayed, *O God, give me your courage. I put my trust in you. Help me to be brave.* I raised my skinny, shaking shoulder. "Give it to me

Pilgrim," I said, mimicking my hero, John Wayne. *He isn't afraid of shots or anything.*

"My poor, sick girl," Aunt Ruthie said sympathetically. "You're so brave to bare your arm for an injection. I'm afraid this injection needs to go into your backside. The injection will be more comfortable for you there. I'll be right back with your medicine."

Yikes. My backside doesn't want an injection. Pete said getting a shot would be easier than giving a speech. What does he know? He's not lying here waiting to get a shot in his backside. Pete would say, 'No sweat, Carol Ann. Just turn over and close your eyes. You've got it made in the shade.' I want to hear Pete yell, APRIL FOOLS, like he did before.

I want Pete to rescue me with his KID COURAGEOUS cape that he wore when we were little kids. Once, he rescued me from a big, scary rooster. If I don't cry when I get this shot, will Pete call me KID COURAGEOUS?

Then my feverish mind pictured Aunt Ruthie's medicine as an atom-sized Mighty Mouse swooping inside my veins. With his cape flying, he'd punch out the bad guys: germs, bacteria, and polio. Mighty Mouse Medicine made it here to save the day. My aunt trusted the medicine from Cutter Labs. I would trust it, too.

"I'm ready, Aunt Ruthie," I whispered then gulped down my fear. "I'll be brave and hold real still for you." As I turned over very slowly, I heard *that* sound. The sound that always sent shivers down my spine. *Yikes. Some unlucky kid in our family is getting a shot, and…it's me!*

Plink. Plink. Ping.

Chapter Twelve

Glad To Be Back

I opened my eyes and looked around. Sunlight streamed into my bedroom. The pink, ruffled curtains fluttered playfully at the open window. I lifted my arms and stretched. *Is my neck still stiff?* I wiggled my head up and down then back and forth. No, my neck feels fine. *Are my legs crippled? Can I still walk?* I kicked off my covers.

Bang, pop, whack. Noisy kids played nearby on the sofa in my bedroom.

I wiggled my toes, moved my legs over the edge of the bed, stood up, and took a step. *My legs still work! Everything works. Thank You, God, for answering our prayers!*

BRUMMM, BRUMMM, BRUMMM. Hawk's Ride roared from next door.

Baking smells teased my nose. My stomach growled like Mr. Chester's puppy. *When did I eat last and what's that light? Oh, it's just the flickering from the television.*

"Here I am to save the day," sang Mighty Mouse from the TV behind the sofa.

"Here I am to see the day," I sang out from my bed. "Where is everyone?" Kathleen, Gail, and Pete popped up from behind the sofa.

"You're back, Carol Ann," said Pete as he jumped over the sofa's back.

"Did I go someplace?" I asked.

"Yeah, you went to Germsville then Dreamland. You finally landed on Cloud 9. You got so sick, you slept all week," said Pete. "Today is April 30th."

"Yikes. I missed a whole week? What germs did I get?" I asked.

Kathleen said, "We thought you had polio. You scared us. We had to wear white masks. You got all shivery, and sweaty, and sick."

Gail said, "I got scared that you got polio outta the gutter."

"Did I get polio?" I asked in a shaky voice as I wiggled my legs again.

"NO!" said Pete. "Dr. Ruth said you had strep throat, tonsillitis, and maybe even rheumatic fever. You bravely took a scary shot! You've got a lot of courage."

"I did take that shot. God gave me courage. I took the shot to get well. It only hurt for a second. Pete, you once said a shot was just a sting. That's so true. Anyone can take a tiny sting on the skin."

"You were sooo brave, Carol Ann," said Gail. She leaned on the sofa back and said, "You asked for medicine to make you well. You were cour-age-a-nous."

Kathleen said, "We're very proud of you."

Pete said, "You're the real KID COURAGEOUS! Before

Dr. Ruth gave you the shot, she told us you said, 'I can do this, Aunt Ruthie, 'cause Pete says I'm the bravest girl in the whole, wide world.' Then you lifted your pajama sleeve to get ready."

"I said that?" I asked.

"Something like that," Pete answered with a smile.

"Pete, you're such a liar. Aunt Ruthie never told you that. I got that shot in my back side," I said and blushed. "My aunt talked me through it. As long as I knew what to expect, the shot didn't hurt that much and took only a second."

"Gee, Carol Ann, you sound like an expert on shots," Pete said. "I hope I never get to be an expert. I like liquid medicine that is given on a spoon and not by a needle."

"Don't we all," I said. "By the way, thanks again for praying for me. God answered your prayer and made me well."

"He sure did. God heard me when I got on my knees," Pete said. "While you slept and tried to get well, you prayed, and cried, and talked."

I pulled up my pillow to lean back on it. My sisters bounced to a cartoon tune, then chattered like chipmunks. Mom's washing machine revved into spin cycle. The curtains fluttered at the window. I listened for howling but didn't hear any.

"I dreamed my worst dream of all on the day of Mary Jane's birthday party," I said. "I felt so sick then I found myself in a world ruled by your sister. Everything looked pink. Atom bombs blew up when your sister banged her cast on stuff."

"That sounds like Mary Jane alright. She acts like that even when it's not a dream," said Pete.

"I carried Hey Pup everywhere I went. Mary Jane wanted him, so she tried to get him from me. I tried to protect Hey Pup from her and some very, scary characters."

"That's what you and I have done all month," said Pete.

"In my dream, I wouldn't let Mary Jane have him. I promised to protect him…but I didn't. I escaped into a cave and left him behind. The dream was so real that I'm sure the puppy is gone forever. I'm the worst kind of coward. I didn't help my furry friend."

"That's not true, Carol Ann," Pete said. "I'm sure he's fine. We've been so busy, I didn't notice he wasn't around all week. It was only a dream."

"I plugged up his escape route that day of the dream. I was too sick to watch him. I thought he'd be safe with Mr. Chester," I admitted with a teary voice. "Hey Pup's beady, black eyes looked so sad that day. I'm afraid we'll never see him again."

"Don't worry, Carol Ann," said Pete. "Hey Pup's a strong puppy, and Mr. Chester isn't totally heartless. He feeds his animals. I'll check on the little rascal today."

"You will? Thanks, Pete. Did you make it over here everyday?" I asked.

"I walked over everyday after school. I played games with the kids and gave your mom a break. I didn't see the puppy that whole time. I was so scared about you, I forgot about him. Your mom made me cookies for helping her," said Pete

"So you had ulterior motives. I'll watch Carol Ann for cookies," I said.

"I ate cookies as a bonus. I would've helped for nothing," Pete defended himself.

"I know that, Pete," I said, smiling. "Thanks."

"Everyone took care of you," he said. "Watching Dr. Ruth fight your illness illuminated my mind. Your fever rose so high, I prayed you wouldn't die. Then the medicine made you better. In your sleep, you mumbled about atom bombs, the birthday party, Tim, giant candles, 'don't be afraid,' The Cruisers, Hey Pup, and neon letters that said Charter something."

"The letters said Cutter not Charter," I said. "Remember the Cutter Laboratories package that Aunt Ruthie got? That box had medicine in it that saved my life."

"I heard Dr. Ruth say that luckily she ordered only penicillin from them and not the polio vaccine, like she wanted too," said Pete.

"I thought Aunt Ruthie gave me a polio vaccine. Everyone whispered that I had polio, because I had so many polio symptoms," I said.

Pete answered, "We're supposed to get the vaccine, so we don't get polio, not *after* we get polio. Anyway, good thing you didn't get that Cutter polio vaccine."

"Why, what was wrong with it?" I asked.

Gail popped up from the sofa and said, "The vaccine got taminated."

"The word is contaminated," said Pete. "Mom read in the newspaper that last Wednesday, April 27, the Surgeon General recalled Cutter's vaccine. Their vaccine contained live virus. A lot of kids got polio from it. My mom worried that you got some."

"Yikes," I said. "I heard Uncle Charlie tell Aunt Ruthie to wait and not order any of the vaccine. I'm sure glad that she listened to him."

"Yeah, me too," said Pete.

"While I slept on Cloud 9, did you have any more trouble from The Cruisers?"

"Nope, we didn't have any more trouble from them and we won't," said Pete. "Butch's Midnight Blue Merc had engine trouble. Someone told Hawk that the Merc's engine blew up and stopped running. The Cruisers can't cruise without a car. They'll have to cruise around town on bicycles like Ernie does."

I noticed something for the first time. "Get well" cards filled my bedroom. They sat on my nightstand. Tape attached them to the wall. Some cards hung like a garland across my window and shimmied in the breeze.

"Wow," I said. "Where did the cards come from?"

"From all your visitors, Miss Popular," Pete answered. "Mary Jane even brought you a card. Look over there at the card covered in pink flowers."

"I thought I dreamed about Mary Jane's visit," I said. "Did she kneel down, hand me a card, and say, 'I hope you get well. Thanks for the cool view finder toy.'"

"Yep, my sister did that," said Pete. "The hospital mask fit her perfectly and would have looked more perfect in pink."

"I had some really scary dreams about Mr. Chester. In one dream, voices on the television sounded like the actors in *The Hurricane* movie starring Jon Hall."

"They were. We watched *The Hurricane* flick," said Pete. "Courageous Jon Hall strapped Dorothy Lamour to a huge tree. He saved her life and some other lives, too."

"In my dream, Mr. Chester stepped out of *The Hurricane* movie and into my bedroom. He sat on Kathleen's bed. He looked grody, but he didn't smell bad. I shivered all over, when he got close to me. I stared up at his wrinkled, whiskery face. A beaky nose stuck out under Mr. Chester's caterpillar eyebrows."

"You didn't have a nightmare, Carol Ann," said Pete. "Mr. Chester visited you."

"His visit was real?" I asked. "I thought he was a nightmare. His gray, scraggly hair stuck straight up in the air. His boney, claw-like fingers reached out . . . and handed me a card. His gravelly voice grated, "Get well soon." Then he limped away on his crutch.

"Mr. Chester did visit you," Pete said, again. "Kathleen worried that he left cooties on her bed. She checked out her bedspread with a magnifying glass like a detective."

"Did Mr. Chester really leave me a card?" I asked Pete as I looked around.

He pointed. "The card's sitting on your nightstand. Be ready for bad news."

I picked it up and opened the envelope. A pretty bouquet of flowers decorated the front of the card. Under the flowers, some typed words said, 'Get Well Wishes.'

"Are there chickens on it?" Pete asked.

"No, just some pretty flowers," I choked out. "The typed words inside say: 'Sending you thoughts of comfort, well being, and love. Hope you are well soon.'"

"Like wow!" Pete exclaimed. "That's nice. Mr. Chester seemed so heartless."

"There's some scratchy handwriting across the bottom of the card," I said. "Listen while I read the handwritten words out loud."

"Get well soon. I'm glad you don't have polio. I didn't want a spunky kid like you to end up like me. Sincerely, Thomas Chester."

"Wow," said Pete. "Mr. Chester has a heart after all!"

"That's so sweet," I sniffed and put the special card down on my nightstand. "Mr. Chester does have a heart. Hey Pup should be okay with him. I'll miss that pesky puppy."

"You won't have to miss him, Carol Ann," said Pete.

"Is that because someone cleared away the rock and dirt I piled over pup's escape route?" I asked. "You mean I won't have to miss him when he visits our yard."

"You won't ever have to miss him," said Pete. "Mr. Chester wanted me to give you something. It's a surprise." Pete walked out of my bedroom and returned a moment later with a cloth-covered basket. He set it on my lap. The basket shook like an earthquake.

"Open it, Carol Ann," said Pete. "It's a good surprise."

"It better be," I said as I yanked off the cloth. Out of the shaking, quaking basket popped…Hey Pup. "Hi there, buddy! Did Mr. Chester drop you off for the day to surprise me? I'm so glad to see you and that you're okay." I patted his white and tan head.

"I told you the pup was okay," said Pete. "But Hey Pup didn't just drop by for a surprise visit. He's here to stay! Mr. Chester wants you to have him *forever*!"

"He does?" I asked. "I get to keep Mr. Chester's puppy forever? Like wow! Mr. Chester is the best! Having this pup is an answer to my prayers!"

Woof, woof, woof. "Hey Pup agrees with you about the prayer," said Pete. "Mr. Chester told me that a spunky kid like you needed to own a spunky puppy like Hey Pup. Mr. Chester also said he was really tired of chasing the puppy around."

Hey Pup tipped his head, so a droopy ear dropped on one side. *Sniff, sniff.* I picked him up and snuggled him on my shoulder. His slobbery puppy licks kissed my cheek.

"Hey Pup! That tickles," I laughed. The pup just licked my cheek some more.

"What are you gonna call the pup now that he's yours?" asked Pete. "He needs a cool name like Rover, or Shep, or Spot, or Toughie."

"What am I gonna call him?" I asked. "He's got a name. It's Hey Pup. I like it." I looked down at the precious puppy.

"You like your name, don't you little buddy?"

"That's his new name," said Pete. "You just said it. I heard you say it."

"No, I didn't," I laughed. "You're hearing things. Did you catch a germ from "Germsville" that causes you to hear things that people don't say?"

"I heard you call him 'little buddy,'" said Pete excitedly. "That's the perfect name for the puppy. We'll call him…Buddy…like in Buddy the Beagle. That's a cool name."

"Hmmmm…Buddy. Like in Buddy the Beagle. Hmmmm," I thought out loud. I lifted up the puppy and looked into his beady eyes. "What do you think, pup? Should we change your name to Buddy?" The pup wiggled his head up and down while he wagged his tail. "I think he likes the new name. Welcome home…Buddy."

"Like crazy, like wow!" said Pete. "Buddy's here to stay."

Mom shuffled into my room carrying a tray. "I'm glad you're awake and sitting up. Are you hungry?" She asked as she moved the basket to put the tray on my lap. "Put the pup back in the basket for now. He'll need lots of care, but he's *awfully* cute."

"Thanks, Mom, for letting Buddy move in with us. Pete and I will take good care of him. And, yes, I'm starving." I looked down at crackers and cheese, tomato soup, cherry gelatin, and homemade chocolate chip cookies. "Thanks for all my favorites."

"I hope you're in a sharing mood," said Pete. "Those cookies look unreal."

I looked at my food, then up at Pete. "They do look good, so leave me one."

Woof, woof, woof. Buddy stood up in his basket. *Sniff, sniff, sniff.* His puppy body bounced up and down like a yo-yo. Pete produced a puppy treat from his pocket and said, "Sit, Buddy." The pup sat down and waited patiently for a doggie biscuit. Pete put the treat in Buddy's mouth. *Crunch, crunch, crunch.*

I laughed as Pete stuffed a warm, delicious, chocolate chip cookie treat into his mouth and mumbled, "Glad you're back, Kid Courageous. You have a lot of courage, Carol Ann. That's why I have another surprise for you." Pete handed me a bundle of red fabric.

"What's this?" I asked as I opened the fabric to see Pete's old cape. Bold black letters spelled out **KID COURAGEOUS**. "Pete, this is your cape from years ago!"

"I searched for it and found it in some old stuff," said Pete. "I think you deserve to wear it now. Put it on. By the way, Hawk said that a kid as brave as you deserved a ride in his '37 Ford. Your mom said a very, slow ride would be okay when you're stronger. And Buddy can ride along, too."

"I'd love to ride in Hawk's Ride with you and Buddy," I said as I put on Pete's precious KID COURAGEOUS cape. Then I picked up one of Mom's cookies from the tray. "I'm glad to be back. I'm glad to own a precious puppy named Buddy. I'm glad you're my friend. I'm glad that God healed me with Aunt Ruthie's medicine; I'm glad this scary spring is over; and I'm really glad to be done with yikes and stings and a shot pot that pings!"

"Hey, boss rhyme, Carol Ann," said Pete. His cookie-stuffed mouth smiled at me.

"Thanks," I said and bit into a warm, gooey chocolate chip cookie. *Yum.*

Crunch, crunch, crunch. Ahwooooooooooooooooooo!

The End

Epilogue

The United States suffered its first great polio epidemic in 1916. Affecting primarily children, thousands died and numerous more were left paralyzed. In 1921, future American president Franklin D. Roosevelt became one of polio's victims.

In January 1938, during his second term in the office of the president, Roosevelt established the National Foundation for Infantile Paralysis. The foundation was made up of scientists and volunteers with the sole purpose of beating out polio.

The Foundation's annual fundraising drive became known as the March of Dimes. With funding from the March of Dimes, the greatest fundraising effort ever undertaken by private citizens for polio vaccine development and research, Dr.

Jonas Salk was able to run the first field trials of a new polio vaccine on over one million schoolchildren in 1954.

Although the field trials and possible vaccine were encouraging, polio continued to terrify the nation until the spring of 1955. It was then when Dr. Salk announced the polio vaccine was successful. The new vaccine didn't cure polio, but Dr. Salk's vaccine kept people from getting the dreaded disease.

Even after the Cutter Laboratory scare, many children and adults went on to receive good polio vaccine and their lives were spared. The American government set up strict rules for drug companies in their handling of the polio vaccine. Dr. Salk gave careful instructions for drug companies to follow so they didn't produce batches of polio vaccine with live viruses in them that could harm the public.

Dr. Jonas Salk was a hero in America and around the world. Incredibly, Dr. Salk never got a patent on his vaccine. Instead, he freely gave his polio vaccine formula to any pharmaceutical company that owned the equipment to safely produce it.

News broadcaster Edward R. Murrow interviewed Dr. Jonas Salk and asked him, "Dr. Salk, who owns the patent on this vaccine?"

Dr. Salk answered, "The polio vaccine belongs to the people. There is no patent. Could you patent the sun?"

In the years since Dr. Jonas Salk discovered the polio vaccine, millions of adults and children in America and around the world have been safely vaccinated against the poliovirus. Cases of polio are extremely rare and mostly in countries that do not vaccinate their population. Groups like The World Health Organization and Rotary Club International still work to eradicate polio in developing nations.

A grateful world continues to give thanks to Dr. Jonas Salk and his team of scientists for their tireless effort to isolate the dreaded poliovirus and create a safe and effective vaccine to prevent polio.

Carol Ann with her dad;
Aunt Ruthie's house and
the chicken car in the
background.

Carol Ann at age 11.

Dad
(Harry Hartnell)

The Hartnell cousins on Easter. Back row, from left: Gail, Kathleen, Uncle Nat's two daughters, Sandy and Pamela, and Carol Ann; front row - Cathie McCammon

EASTER

Mom (Jeanne Hartnell) with daughters. From left - Kathleen, Gail, and Carol Ann.

From left, cousins Cathie and Little Charlie McCammon with Carol Ann, Kathleen, and Gail, sitting in the blow-up pool in their yard.

Dr. Jonas Salk, center, with Uncle Charlie (Dr. Charles McCammon), left, and Basil O'Connor, president of the National Foundation of Infantile Paralysis.

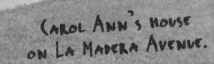

CAROL ANN'S HOUSE ON LA MADERA AVENUE.

FAMILY FUN.
Front row, left to right —
neighbor boy, Gail,
Carol Ann;
back row — Cathie,
Aunt Ruthie, Little
Charlie, Uncle Charlie,
and Kathleen.

Downtown El Monte, CA
1950's

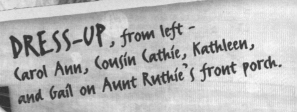

DRESS-UP, from left –
Carol Ann, Cousin Cathie, Kathleen,
and Gail on Aunt Ruthie's front porch.

Uncle Charlie standing on
the driveway, probably
waiting for us girls to
hurry up.

CHERRYLEE SCHOOL

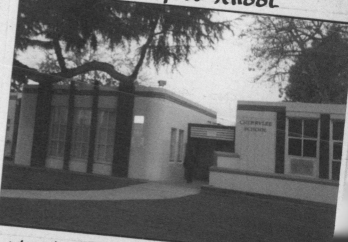

where Carol Ann and her friends attended.

Polio: An American Story by David M. Oshinsky; Oxford University Press, 2005.

Polio Voices: An Oral History from the American Polio Epidemics and Worldwide Eradication Efforts (The Praeger Series on Contemporary Health and Living) by J.K. Silver; Praeger, 2007.

The 1950s (American Popular Culture Through History) by William H. Young and Nancy K. Young; Greenwood, 2004.

America in the 1950s (Decades of American History) by Charles Wills; Chelsea House Publications, 2005.

The 1950s: Music (Century Kids) by Dorothy Hoobler and Tom Hoober; Millbrook Press, 2001.

March of Dimes
http://www.marchofdimes.com/

Rotary International / The Rotary Foundation
http://www.rotary.org/

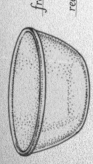

from the kitchen of Mrs. Hartnell

recipe for Yummy Chocolate Chip Cookies

---

ingredients

½ cup butter (one stick)
1½ cups packed brown sugar
2 eggs
1 teaspoon vanilla extract
2¼ cups flour (all-purpose)
1 teaspoon baking soda
1 teaspoon salt
2 cups semi-sweet chocolate chips
1 cup chopped pecans (optional)

---

instructions

Heat the oven to 350°. In a large bowl, combine butter, brown sugar, eggs, and vanilla extract. Mix together until fluffy. Add flour (one cup at a time), baking soda, and salt. Mix well. Stir in chocolate chips, and if desired, pecans. Drop rounded tablespoons of dough, 2 inches apart, onto ungreased cookie sheets. Bake for 8-10 minutes. When cookies are browned, remove them from the oven and cool on cookie sheets for 2 minutes. With a metal spatula, carefully move each cookie to a wire rack or place on a brown paper bag to cool completely. Makes 4 dozen yummy cookies.